"With you around everything most things difficult—if not impossible!"

"My, that's some effect I have on you," he mocked, "but if it's any consolation, the feeling's quite mutual."

"Ever since I was a child you've played cat and mouse with me, either tearing strips off me for my alleged crimes and telling me what a moron I am, or shriveling me with your sarcasm—and nothing's changed!" exploded Lucy.

"Correction—some things haven't changed. You're still the petulant, spoiled brat you always were—and the only thing that's changed there is that nowadays you come more attractively packaged!"

"Packaged?"

KATE PROCTOR is part Irish and part Welsh, though she spent most of her childhood in England and several years of her adult life in Central Africa. Now divorced, she lives just outside London with her two cats, Florence and Minnie—presented to her by her two daughters who live fairly close by.

Having given up her career as a teacher on her return to England, Kate now devotes most of her time to writing. Her hobbies include crossword puzzles, bridge and, at the moment, learning Spanish.

Books by Kate Proctor

KATE PROCTOR

Bittersweet Yesterdays

Harlequin Books

TORONTO • NEW YORK • LONDON
AMSTERDAM • PARIS • SYDNEY • HAMBURG
STOCKHOLM • ATHENS • TOKYO • MILAN
MADRID • WARSAW • BUDAPEST • AUCKLAND

ISBN 0-373-11710-8

BITTERSWEET YESTERDAYS

CHAPTER ONE

'YOU'RE joking, of course! Me? Your secretary?' Lucy Preston flashed her stepbrother a look of horrified defiance across the huge, leather-topped desk separating them—a look completely wasted, it infuriated her to find, on Mark Waterford, who, having delivered his tersely worded bombshell, had turned his attention to one of the telephones beside him and began dialling a number.

'Yes, you—my secretary,' he snapped. 'And I wasn't asking your opinion, I was simply telling you that's to be your position for the time being.' With barely a pause, he launched into a rapid flow of French as his call connected, leaving Lucy leaning back heavily in her chair, her teeth almost grinding with fury.

She was twenty-three years old, she fumed to herself—not the accident-prone fifteen-year-old who had been abandoned to Mark Waterford's despotic—not to mention vociferously reluctant—mercies virtually from the day her mother had married his father, James Waterford. *The* James Waterford, she reminded herself acerbically, of the fabled Waterford Consortium.

Lucy glowered across the desk at the man on the telephone. At fifteen she had been smitten by the most devastating of infatuations for her then twenty-two-year-old stepbrother—with his careless sophistication and rakish good looks he had seemed like the embodiment of her every romantic dream.

Her eyes narrowed slightly as they moved from the
glossy dark thickness of his hair to the almost chiselled
perfection of his features. She frowned with the effort
of trying to pinpoint exactly what it was about him that
drew women to him in their droves. Perhaps it was that
intriguing blend of harshness and sensuality that was
there, not only in his extraordinarily good looks but also
in his personality. Or perhaps they were attracted by the
broad streak of tyranny in him, to which she had been
subjected, on and off, for the past eight years, she mused
scathingly; if that was the case, they should all be certified, she decided, tensing perceptibly as he terminated
the call.

Mark Waterford rose to his feet and proceeded to
stretch. He was a tall man, well over six feet, and there
wasn't a square ounce of flesh on his magnificently pro-
portioned body. He lowered his arms when he had finished stretching, his powerful shoulders flexing beneath
the dazzling white of his shirt, then he returned to his
seat. He gazed across at the slim figure of his stepsister,
a dismissive impatience in the cold blue of his eyes.

'Well, don't lounge around here looking as though
you're about to doze off,' he snapped. 'I suggest you
get your bits and pieces moved into my reception office.'

Lucy, who had been doing some rapid mental arith-
metic and had come up with answers she found depressing, glowered over at him while biting back her
inexpressible views as to what he and the entire Waterford
Consortium could do regarding what she considered her
enforced connections with them.

'It's hardly likely to do much for your image,' she stalled, 'promoting the typing pool's equivalent of the village idiot to your secretary.'

'It so happens that I've decided it's high time something was done about that village idiot routine of yours,' he retorted coldly. 'And it's a pose you'll find yourself dropping pretty damn quickly around me, I can assure you.'

'Oh, I see,' gushed Lucy, glaring balefully at him. 'You've decided to have another bash at furthering my education, have you?'

He tilted his large frame back in the leather swivel chair as he gave her a look of fastidious forbearance with which she was all too familiar.

'Your education—or, to be more precise, your appalling lack of it—is and never has been of the slightest interest to me,' he informed her with exaggerated patience. 'But the unfortunate fact that you happen to be a peripheral member of my family——'

'I'm *not* a member of your precious family!' exploded Lucy. 'The fact that my mother is married to your father has nothing to do with me! And another thing,' she continued, every single one of her pent-up frustrations clamouring to have a say, 'unlike you, I happened to have a completely open mind about their marriage at the time—I could hardly have been expected to foresee that my mother would lose her reason and waltz off and leave me at your mercy. I'd have been better off if she'd dumped me on the streets!'

'Here we go again,' he groaned, rolling his eyes in disbelief. 'You're like a stuck record. Damn it, on the streets is probably where you'd have ended up if it hadn't been for my father!' His eyes blazed their fury across the desk at her. 'Your mother was up to her eyeballs in debt when she married him——'

'You're the one like a stuck record,' Lucy practically screamed at him. 'She didn't marry him for his money! For heaven's sake, how much convincing do you need? They've been happily married for eight years now and you still accuse——'

'I'm accusing no one of anything,' he cut in coldly. 'I was merely pointing out the facts. And another fact is that I wouldn't have been left here with you virtually on my hands if you'd behaved like any normal child and gone with them to the States as they wanted—so don't give me any more of your sanctimonious hogwash about how open-minded you were about them marrying!'

'I was *fifteen*, for heaven's sake!' shrieked Lucy indignantly. 'It was only four years since my own father had died . . . the last thing I wanted was to be uprooted from England and all my friends.'

'And how did you behave when you got your own way?' he demanded witheringly.

'I *didn't* get my own way,' she protested angrily, wondering why she had even bothered—no one had ever attempted to look at her turbulent teenage years from her point of view and Mark was the last person to do so now. 'I was dragged from the school I knew and loved, and from all my friends, and dumped in a snooty boarding-school where I was a complete misfit!'

'Damn it, how else could they have left you in England without sending you to boarding-school?' he demanded impatiently. 'And the fact that you couldn't stand the place was hardly a reason for attempting to burn it to the ground.'

Lucy gritted her teeth and said nothing—what was the point in saying anything now when it had been her own obstinate pride that had condemned her all those years ago?

When Mark had been summoned to the school from his studies at Cambridge it had been impossible for her to judge which had hurt her most: the object of her secret adoration's arriving with a sultry blonde in tow, or the crushing words with which he had greeted her.

'This is all I need—you taking up arson!'

In her hurt confusion she had been unable to utter a single word. The fury that had erupted in him as he had taken her silence as total confirmation of her guilt had spawned a brainstorm of furious indignation in her which had eventually resulted in her screaming at him that she would make sure the place burned to a cinder if she had to remain there. Her immediate expulsion had removed any likelihood of her actually carrying out that mindless threat—but what had hurt her even more deeply was that her own mother, loving and concerned though she had been, had never once appeared to question her guilt either.

'My father should have put his foot down then and made sure you stayed with them in the States until you were fit to be let loose on the world,' continued Mark ruthlessly. 'But no—once you turned sixteen you got your own way and returned to England to——'

'Only because the American education system is so different,' interrupted Lucy with hot indignation. 'There was no way I could suddenly fit in there.'

'Yet you didn't have much success fitting in here either,' he pointed out unkindly. 'How many different courses was it you started on, only to drop out of?'

'And I'm sure you don't consider you played any part in that, do you?' she lashed out at him with all the passionate resentment of her teenage years. 'I was doing well and really enjoying the art foundation course at Kingston——'

'Yes—so much that you dropped out of it after barely a year,' he jeered.

'And you know perfectly well why!' she accused hotly. 'Because of those two harpies you farmed me out with! They made my life an absolute misery. If I wasn't back at their place by eight, they used to call the police. I must have been the only art student in the entire country who had to be home by eight—weekends included!'

'Lucy, I simply haven't the time to sit here being subjected to a blow-by-blow account of your delinquent youth,' he drawled in tones of bored disdain, sliding back the cuff of his shirt to display a slim gold watch at his darkly haired wrist.

He was a gloriously hairy man, she suddenly found herself thinking. Not in any way abnormally so—there were some men who looked positively ape-like, whereas Mark was... She pulled herself up abruptly, experiencing an uncomfortable churning sensation in the pit of her stomach as she remembered the precise moment she had made the discovery as to his hirsuteness or otherwise. It was one morning during the two weeks when he had had no option but to put her up at his flat and during which he had made it starkly clear she was the most unwelcome of guests. Having believed him to be out, she had gone racing into his bedroom to investigate the alarming sounds emanating from it . . . on reflection, she realised the girl sharing his bed had probably felt every bit as disconcerted as she had. She glared across the desk at Mark, his unconcerned laughter as he had ordered her from the room all those years ago once again ringing in her ears.

'You were the one who brought up the subject,' she informed him, her tone suddenly switching to ominous sweetness. 'And while we're on it—perhaps you'd care to cast your mind back to those two ghastly weeks I was forced to spend at your flat.'

'*You* were forced?' he queried with supercilious indignation. 'My God, that's rich! I reckon I deserved a medal simply for having let my father talk me into allowing you to stay there!'

'No, if you deserved a medal for anything, it was your stamina as a stud—as far as I can remember, you had a different woman every night, and that was hardly an example to be setting for an impressionable teenager, now was it, Mark?'

'Lucy, darling, your terminology is, to put it mildly, unfortunate,' he murmured through clenched teeth. 'I might have seen different women every night, but . . .' He broke off with an eloquent shrug that brought the colour racing to her cheeks. 'But I have to admit that one woman did spend the night there during your stay,' he conceded off-handedly. 'And I also admit that it was wrong of me to allow her to do so—just as it was wrong of me to credit you with enough intelligence not to come barging in on us. And as for your picture of yourself as an impressionable teenager—I'd be more inclined to de-

scribe as delinquent a sixteen-year-old who decides to
take a joy-ride in an extremely expensive car—especially
one who wrecks it before she's even managed to get it
out of the garage.'

Lucy leapt to her feet, beside herself with fury. Yes,
she had almost wrecked his precious car—but that was
only half the story. And, as always, he hadn't even attempted to find out the other half!

'I take it you're now off to get your things and move
them into your new office,' he murmured tauntingly,
having beaten her to the door, which he now nonchalantly barred.

There was consternation as well as defiance in Lucy's
wide-spaced blue eyes as they rose to those of the man
towering over her. As always, when she stood this close
to him, she felt as though her five and a half feet of
height had shrunk to four. And that wasn't the only effect
he had on her. The amount of male attention she received was more than enough to confirm that she was
an attractive woman; all too often the slender curva-
ceousness of her lithe young body and the wholesome
loveliness of her features brought her attention she could
well do without, yet at this very moment she felt like a
frumpy fifteen-year-old.

Rattled by these confidence-sapping sensations
flooding her, she made to flick her cornsilk, shoulder-
length hair behind her ears—a gesture she resorted to
without even being aware of it whenever she felt nervous
or threatened—only to find that today was one of those
days she had decided to tie it back.

'Yes—I'll move my things into that office, but only
because I haven't any choice!' she flung at him, furious

with herself for the way she was feeling. 'But I warn you, I'm sure there's a law against what you're doing to me—and when I find out what it is, I'll ... I'll sue you through every court there is!'

'You plan to sue me for plucking you from what amounts to a typing pool and making you my secretary?' he murmured in wonderment, the laughter colouring his words incensing her.

'You know perfectly well what I mean!' she raged. 'Every time I've tried applying for other jobs, you've made sure I didn't get them—I don't know how, probably through some business mafia you belong to, but I *know* you have!'

'I suppose it would never occur to you that other potential employers found you lacking in some way?' he taunted.

'If that's the case, why do you want me as your secretary?' she demanded triumphantly.

'I have my reasons,' he murmured enigmatically. 'Now, would you mind——?'

'Silly me—of course you have!' exclaimed Lucy, her eyes widening in indignation as a thought suddenly struck her. 'You've been here how long—four months? And you've been through secretaries like a dose of salts! Dear me, now I really am getting the picture! Let's see, two Waterford offices in the States, four on the Continent— and possibly sundry others dotted around the world I've never even heard of—and you've alley-catted your way through all of them!' She could tell by the thunderous expression on his face that she should stop, but the words kept coming. 'And now you've hit London—and at last it's dawned on you that business and the sort of pleasure you revel in simply don't mix. No wonder you're prepared to put up with me as a secretary—it probably wouldn't even bother you if I couldn't type.'

It astounded her how quickly he had moved. One minute they were facing one another in combat, the next she was locked in his arms, the muscled hardness of his body imprinting itself down the length of hers as though the clothing had been stripped from her.

'But what if you've got it all wrong, Lucy?' he murmured with threatening softness. 'What if I've decided to move in on you... and really finish off your education?'

She had never been this close to him; never experienced the mind-sapping chaos of excitement of being in his arms.

'I... you... I've already been thoroughly educated in that particular department, thank you very much,' she stammered with childlike guilelessness, her heart hammering as though it would burst against the wall of his chest.

'What a relief it is to hear that,' he whispered, his head lowering as though in slow motion towards hers. 'That means we can dispense with all these boring preliminaries and get down to the really advanced business.'

And there was nothing in the least preliminary about his kiss. His mouth possessed hers with a practised thoroughness that startled her into a complete lack of resistance to the probing invasion of his tongue. But it wasn't simply the instantly intoxicating effect of his mouth on hers that she had to contend with, it was also the debilitating excitement caused by the hands that had somehow found their way beneath her sweater and to which her flesh responded as though to high voltage, intensely pleasurable blasts of electricity.

These were *Mark's* lips burning against hers with such swiftly soaring passion, her crazily spinning senses tried to warn her; and Mark's hands moving with such inflammatory effect against her flesh and making her feel more acutely conscious of being a woman than she ever had in her life before.

'No!' She tore herself free, staggering backwards from him, her hands rising to cover her face in a gesture of sheer panic as she battled to regain her senses.

It had taken all the strength of will she possessed to drag herself free from the mesmerising spell of his touch, and it was the mere fact that it had been necessary for her to conjure up such a strength that was terrifying the wits out of her.

'Lucy, don't you dare go throwing a wobbly on me,' warned Mark, his voice oddly strained despite the aggression in its tone. 'I'm perfectly aware that I stepped way out of line—and I'm sorry.'

She spread her fingers open against her face, peeping through them at him, but far too wary of what her own voice might betray for her to dare attempt speaking.

'You're just going to have to learn to stop riling me like that,' he exploded accusingly, 'especially now you'll be working for me.'

Lucy's hands dropped from her face in a fury of indignation that swept all other considerations from her mind.

'That's a great apology—telling me it's my fault for riling you,' she exclaimed angrily. 'Since when have I ever opened my mouth and not managed to rile you?

And now you order me to work in close proximity with
you! What are you—some sort of masochist? I haven't
the first idea what being a secretary entails, but I'm sure
that'll make it all the more fun for you!'

'What the hell's that supposed to mean?' he roared.
'For God's sake, one of the few courses you managed
to survive was at that ludicrously exclusive—not to
mention extortionately expensive—secretarial college you
went to!'

'Yes, but you obviously didn't read any of the reports——'

'I wasn't interested in the damned reports—just as long
as they didn't sling you out,' he interrupted harshly. 'I
was under the impression they gave you certificates when
you left,' he added, frowning.

'Yes—one for elementary typing and another for
shorthand at fifty words a minute,' she retorted, knowing
that such information would probably be double-Dutch
to him.

'So—what's the problem?' he enquired, his tone suspicious as his frown deepened.

Lucy opened her mouth to inform him that there were
probably several typists in the company who could type
twice as fast as she had once been able to take down
shorthand—most of which she had probably forgotten
anyway—then had second thoughts. She had taken the
course simply to learn the basic typing skills she felt
would be a useful tool in her ambition to write and for
that reason had never regretted it, but, though her speed
had improved markedly, there was no guaranteeing it
wouldn't collapse with Mark standing over her.

'You can't be that bad,' he muttered, doubt resonant in his tone, 'otherwise you'd have flitted off to another department, as you did with such monotonous regularity when you first started here.'

'You're wrong—I can be that bad,' she informed him with gloating satisfaction. 'Though, to be fair, even though I'm slow, I'm painstakingly accurate when it comes to complicated figure work—that's why they dump all those mind-bogglingly boring specifications and the like on me.'

He gave her a wary, speculative look, pursing his lips as he did so.

Lucy found her eyes drawn irresistibly to his mouth, a strident excitement exploding through her as she relived the sensation of that mouth on hers—not pursed as it was now, as though for a chaste kiss, but open and uninhibited in its hungry exploration. She gave a sharp toss of her head in an attempt to clear it of the madness of such thoughts and felt the colour sting hotly against her cheeks.

'OK—so you're slow but accurate,' exclaimed Mark brusquely, dragging his fingers through his hair with a gesture of weary impatience. 'Lucy, we've really got to do something about clearing the air between us. I know you'll probably not believe this, but I've been meaning to get around to having a talk with you ever since I arrived, but I've simply not found the time.'

Lucy's look of sceptical disbelief was lost on him as he glanced down at his watch.

'Look—let's get your bits and pieces up here, then we can take an early lunch.'

Without waiting for her reply, he strode over to his desk and got his jacket. Lucy watched as he shrugged his broad shoulders into it, her mind racing frantically.

'Well, come along, then,' he urged, opening the door and glowering impatiently as he waited for her to make a move to go through it.

'I . . . Mark, I'm not eating in the staff canteen with you,' she burst out anxiously.

'Who mentioned the canteen? There's a good Italian place round the corner, where they usually manage to find me a table.'

He was the sort of man for whom most restaurants probably always managed to find a table, even if it meant turfing some other poor devil out, thought Lucy resentfully.

'Lucy!'

'Mark, I——'

'Shift yourself!' he snapped, grasping her by the arm and propelling her forcibly through the door.

'I'm perfectly capable of getting my own things,' she hissed at him in the lift, her eyes studiously avoiding his scowling features.

'Are you?'

'Yes! And I——' She broke off with a squeak of protest as she was virtually shoved through the lift doors before they had finished opening. 'Stop treating me like this!' she raged, trying in vain to twist free of his grasp as he marched her towards the general typing offices. 'I was perfectly happy here until you spoiled it all by turning up.' She glanced up at his glacial features as he marched her relentlessly on, her heart sinking as she realised she was going to have to humiliate herself by pleading with him. 'Mark—even you must realise how odd people are going to find this,' she wailed.

'Find what odd?' he demanded.

'For heaven's sake—you're practically God around here! People are bound to——'

She gave a strangled gasp as he halted unexpectedly and spun her round to face him.

'OK, Lucy, spit it out—what exactly is your problem?'

'I...well, if you must know, no one knows you're my stepbrother...well, no one apart from the executives, as far as I know,' she stammered, then added venomously, 'I certainly haven't told anyone!'

Her eyes widened in total disbelief as he began chuckling softly to himself.

'Don't tell me you're actually worried what it might do to your reputation, being seen hob-nobbing with the—"alley-catting" was the term I believe you used—boss. My, that is a problem, sweetheart.'

'Don't you dare call me sweetheart!' she shrieked, then clapped her hand over her mouth, her eyes flying with stricken concern to the door near by and finding it mercifully closed.

'You know,' he murmured with gloating relish, 'I'm sure we could give them a lot to talk about—if I really put my mind to it.'

'Mark...please,' she begged.

There was nothing she wouldn't put past him, and the thought of having to live it down with her colleagues was something that didn't even bear contemplating—especially Sarah Mitson, her closest friend, to whom she still hadn't got around to divulging her complicated relationship to Mark.

'Why, Lucy, sweetheart, I do believe you're grovelling,' he murmured complacently, releasing her and flashing her a wickedly taunting look as he stepped forward and held the door open for her.

Her eyes trained on the rich green carpeting beneath her feet, Lucy entered.

As with all the Waterford London offices, this general typing complex was magnificently equipped and almost lavishly appointed. Though she had no other work experience with which to make comparisons, Lucy had learned from the comments of staff from several of the departments within the company that Waterford's wholly deserved their envied international reputation where staff pay, conditions and, most of all, job satisfaction were concerned. To refer to where she worked, as most did, as a 'typing pool' she knew was a complete misnomer. And it was too to refer to her colleagues simply as typists. Of the six of them, three were graduates, attracted by the company's liberal internal promotion policies and lack of sex discrimination. Two current heads of department had started their careers in this very office. And she was the duffer among them, thought Lucy resignedly as she trudged, head bowed, towards her desk—acutely conscious of Mark close on her heels and the palpably loaded atmosphere permeating the suddenly hushed office.

'My, my—and what have we been up to?' teased Sarah wickedly beneath her breath as Lucy, now scarlet-faced, passed her and halted at her own desk.

She loved Sarah dearly, she thought resignedly, noticing how her friend had openly abandoned all idea of work to gaze with wide-eyed interest on what was going on around her, but there were times, such as right now, when she could happily throttle her.

She dug a large plastic bag out of one of the drawers and then proceded to tip the entire contents of all the drawers into it.

'Heck, Lucy—you haven't been fired, have you?' exclaimed Sarah, her look turning to one of horrified suspicion.

Lucy glanced pleadingly over at her friend, now on her feet and regarding her with a look of shocked indignation, then towards Mark, standing impassively by her desk.

'Of course not—but I'll have to explain later,' she muttered in Sarah's direction, then flashed her an imploring look—when it came to defending her friends, Sarah's normally placid nature could become startlingly aggressive.

'Is that it?' enquired Mark, glancing with open disdain at the overflowing carrier bag Lucy was now hoisting precariously in her arms.

She nodded and, casting what she hoped was a reassuring look in her stunned friend's direction, followed him as he began marching out of the office.

'Hang on a minute, Mark,' she exclaimed when they had almost reached the door, and could have bitten off her tongue for her carelessness in speaking in what, to her colleagues, must have sounded an astounding familiar way to address the supreme boss. 'I've forgotten my coat.'

He turned and faced her, his expression long-suffering. 'OK—wait there while I get it,' he muttered, striding back past her. 'Where is it?'

'I'll get it,' offered one of the other girls, having difficulty keeping her face straight as she raced off, then returned and handed Lucy's coat to a deceptively patient-looking Mark.

'Is that it?' he asked Lucy, in tones of equally deceptive patience as he slung her coat nonchalantly over his shoulder.

She nodded, deciding she could collect her scarf and boots, which she had just that moment remembered, later.

'Come on, then,' he snapped, striding past her, 'we haven't got all day.'

Gritting her teeth, she followed him down the corridor and into the lift, where she maintained a frigid silence which her companion showed no inclination to break on their journey back to his suite of offices.

No wonder she hadn't been able to bring herself to tell even Sarah about her unfortunate connection with the Waterford family, especially not this monster, she fumed resentfully to herself as she entered the office that was to be hers—her pride simply hadn't the stomach for it.

She placed the carrier bag on the desk and tipped its contents on to it.

'Right—now that you've reduced this place to the sort of mess only you would feel at home in, perhaps we can go and eat,' drawled Mark from the doorway, flinging her coat across the room at her as he left to get his own.

Clutching her coat to her, she raced out after him.

'I'll not last five minutes here—so what's the point of my bothering?' she demanded. 'And as for having lunch with you, it's an ordeal I've decided to skip!'

'Damn it, Lucy,' he exclaimed, striding threateningly towards her, 'stop behaving like a spoiled brat—I've told you there are things I need to discuss with you!'

'Perhaps if you stopped treating me like a child I'd——' She broke off in consternation as the memory of how much a woman she had felt in his arms seared suddenly through her.

'You were saying?' he mocked softly, both his words and the disconcertingly predatory gleam in his eyes leaving her in no doubt that he sensed what was going through her mind. 'Lucy, I think we ought to go—before I'm tempted to give you further proof that I no longer regard you as a child.'

CHAPTER TWO

BY THE time they were seated in the restaurant, Lucy was feeling as miserable physically as she was mentally. Without her scarf, a voluminous cashmere wrap which had been a birthday present from her mother and James, she was frozen; and without her boots her feet had been soaked in the rain.

'No wonder you're cold,' said Mark unsympathetically, catching her shiver, despite the warmth surrounding them, as he finished giving their order. 'You're not exactly dressed for December weather.'

'Only because you didn't give me time to get changed into something suitable,' snapped Lucy, acutely conscious of a completely new dimension to the edgy tension she generally experienced in his company, yet unable to pinpoint its cause.

'As your coat was all you claimed to have with you,' he replied in innocent tones, 'I can only assume you're complaining I didn't give you time to go home and change—and that's hardly a reasonable complaint.'

'What did you want to talk to me about?' she demanded wearily. She knew this patronisingly innocent mood of his of old, and it was one that more often than not reduced her to gibbering rage.

'Perhaps I should have ordered you a brandy to warm you up,' he murmured, disregarding her words totally. 'You have, I take it, learned to hold your liquor by now?'

Lucy was mortified to feel her cheeks flame.

'Ha, ha,' she ground out, inwardly squirming. At sixteen she had, quite by accident, managed to get herself well and truly drunk on an innocuous-tasting punch she had unfortunately assumed to be a concoction of nothing but fruit juices.

'How old were you at the time?' enquired Mark, once again displaying that disconcerting knack of reading her mind.

'Sixteen,' snapped Lucy, then rounded on him bitterly. 'And if you hadn't dragged me along to that wretched do, only to dump me in a corner and order me to blend in with the wallpaper, I wouldn't have spent the entire evening drinking in order to relieve the boredom!'

'Is there nothing you've ever done that hasn't been someone else's fault?' he asked, his tone as icy as the eyes contemptuously holding hers across the table as the waiters arrived. 'And just in case you were thinking of replying, don't bother,' he informed her, once they had been served. 'In fact, I'd be grateful if you didn't utter another word until I've finished my entire meal. I've no intention of risking an ulcer by subjecting myself to your petulant outbursts while I'm eating.'

There *was* something different about him, thought Lucy nervously, feeling like a severely reprimanded child. It was around two years since she had spent any time in his company, she mused, and also since his father had handed the entire business empire over to him. And before that there had been a similar gap between their meetings.

She picked at her food half-heartedly, startled to realise how long those gaps had been—not that time had
ever lessened the intensity of the all-out war that had
always existed between them. She frowned, giving an
imperceptible shake of her head as she remembered that
it hadn't always been total war between them. From
around the time she was seventeen and well into her
eighteenth year, they had almost got on well, she realised
with a sharp pang of nostalgia—admittedly they had still
argued, but not with the venom of the earlier years and
certainly not as they were to in the years that followed.
And that strange period, almost of truce, had taken place
during the time when his father had been reassessing the
London offices and when he and her mother had, for
the first time since their marriage, actually lived for a
while in London.

Mark had still been a student, and younger than she
was now, when he had been forced into the role of virtual
guardian to a stroppy fifteen-year-old, and how bitterly
he had resented it, she thought with a curiously tender
pang of understanding. Perhaps it wasn't a coincidence
that the only time they had almost got on was when her
mother and his father had been around to relieve him
of that onerous burden they themselves had placed on
him. It was definitely when James and her mother left
England again that hostilities had flared up between them
with renewed intensity…even though she was old enough
to stand on her own two feet—well, almost—by then.

Her mind still wrestling with such thoughts, she gazed
furtively across the table at her silent companion and in
that instant her mind blanked, only to be filled by
sudden, searing memories of his lips on hers.

For heaven's sake, all he'd done was kiss her, she remonstrated frantically with herself—except that it was so out of character that it had obviously thrown even him. But one thing she could be sure of—if ever he got any inkling of the effect that kiss had had on her, he would use it as a weapon against her without the slightest compunction!

'Would you like coffee?' he asked, finally breaking the silence.

Lucy nodded, her mind still resisting her efforts to clear it of the memories it seemed determined to dwell on.

He summoned a waiter, then didn't speak again until the table was cleared and the coffee served.

'About two and a half years ago, my father underwent major surgery for a stomach disorder,' he then stated quietly.

Lucy looked at him in shocked disbelief.

'Why didn't anyone tell me?' she asked hoarsely.

'Probably because they felt you had enough to contend with at the time—that is, being plastered all over the Press as a gangster's moll.'

'Mark, you know you're not being fair.' As she was still stunned by his disclosure, her protest was mild. 'I hardly knew the man—I just happened to be having lunch with him when he was arrested. And as for it being plastered all over the——'

'Perhaps not here; but it was in the States, where the man was wanted on several charges,' he muttered. 'And you can imagine how it must have speeded my father's recovery once the American Press dug up your link with him and brought his name into it all.'

He wasn't being in the least fair, but Lucy was still too preoccupied by thoughts of her stepfather, of whom she had gradually grown very fond, to react.

'Lucy, you're right—I wasn't being fair,' he sighed. 'But to get back to Dad's operation; by all medical expectations it should have returned him to his old self—but unfortunately it didn't.'

Lucy gazed at him aghast. 'That rumpus I was involved in...are you saying it affected him that badly?'

'Of course I'm not,' he exclaimed, then startled her by giving her a wry grin. 'Though I'd be lying if I said the thought never entered my mind.' His expression reverted to one of seriousness. 'Lucy, don't tell me you didn't find it odd that he should hand over the company to me, and opt out of all involvement with it, so early. It was something he had always intended doing eventually, but certainly not in his early fifties!'

Lucy hoped her expression wasn't betraying her thoughts. She had had one or two thoughts on the subject of James handing over his empire lock, stock and barrel to his son—and none of them in the least charitable towards Mark—but the idea of poor health having any bearing on it simply hadn't entered her head.

'He did it because he realised he lacked the physical stamina to continue. It got so that a full round of golf was more than he could handle—and you know how he is about his golf.'

'This is dreadful,' whispered Lucy, feeling suddenly limp and trembly. 'If only someone had had the sense to tell me. The things I've said to them! I virtually accused them of acting like a couple of couch potatoes! I spent last Christmas with them—at that place they sud-

denly bought in the Seychelles. I just couldn't understand how they could sit around all day playing cards
when there was so much to do there...I feel terrible!'

He gave a small shrug. 'You weren't to know—and
anyway, it doesn't matter. Give him a while and he'll be
back to his old energetic self.'

'What do you mean?'

'One of the reasons he bought that place in the
Seychelles was that he'd had enough of being treated
like some sort of medical specimen by the team that had
originally operated on him. I suppose you couldn't blame
them really. When such relatively routine surgery
produces unheard-of results like that, they're bound to
want to know why. But after the last extensive going-
over they gave him, he'd had enough.'

'Has the climate there cured him or something?' asked
Lucy tentatively.

He laughed as he shook his head. 'I'm afraid not. But
with what they had from the last batch of tests, his
doctors have finally cracked it—and it took some doing.
I've no idea what the medical jargon is, but it appears
Dad's innards aren't quite as they should be according
to the textbooks. It's a minor deviation which, ironi-
cally, wouldn't have affected him a jot had he not had
to have precisely the surgery he did have a couple of
years ago.'

'But they can cure it now they know?'

He nodded. 'Unfortunately it involves another hefty
bout of surgery. But once he's over that, he really will
be back to normal this time.'

'When will he have the operation?'

'In the New Year. In fact, they're flying back to the States the day after New Year and he'll be operated on a day or two later.'

'Mark . . . I'm so glad,' whispered Lucy almost shyly. 'I know I used to say how much I hated him when they were first married . . . I suppose it was a confused sort of loyalty to my own father. But over the years I've grown very fond of him.'

'Loyalty such as that is perfectly understandable,' he muttered. 'It took a long time for me to admit it even to myself, but your mother's the best thing that could have happened to him. After my mother died, he just went to pieces.' He broke off and shifted slightly in his chair, the movement uncharacteristically tense and awkward. 'It was in that state that he ended up married— briefly, thank God—to an archetypal gold-digger. It was unfortunate but inevitable that I should regard your mother as being a similar type.'

It was only when he glanced around and motioned to a waiter to bring more coffee that Lucy realised he had said all he intended. No apology; no admission of any feelings even approaching warmth for the woman who had borne his open hostility with such fortitude—only that grudging statement.

'So why are you telling me all this now?' she asked, anger and resentment simmering within her. 'I'm amazed I haven't been left in total ignorance as usual.'

'This time I intend making sure you stay out of trouble—and with your full co-operation. I don't want anything—and I mean not the slightest thing—causing him any unwarranted stress while he's going through this.'

'And you really expect me to believe you don't blame me for his failure to recover last time?' exploded Lucy bitterly, unable to believe she was being treated like this.

'Your infantile sensibilities aren't of the slightest interest to me,' he drawled, the boredom in his tone complemented by his eyes, which then left her to follow the progress of the extremely attractive woman walking past their table. 'The only thing I'm interested in,' he continued, though apparently having difficulty dragging his eyes temporarily back to Lucy, 'is the next couple of months being as stress-free as possible for my father.'

'Oh, dear,' drawled Lucy, the blood boiling in her as she suspected he had succeeded in making some sort of eye-contact with the woman who, with her companion, had taken a table not quite in her line of vision some-where to the left of theirs. 'It looks as though I'm going to have to say goodbye to my dishy drug baron boy-friend—what a shame.'

The look he gave her was such that for an instant she was scared he was going to lunge across the table and throttle her.

'You come out with remarks like that,' he rasped, controlling himself with patent difficulty, 'and yet you wonder why I feel the need to make sure I've got you right where I can keep close watch on you.'

'I take it you're referring to my new secretarial po-sition,' exclaimed Lucy with a dismissive laugh. 'I hope you realise that any day now you'll be kicking yourself for not having hung on to one of those you so rashly discarded.'

'There was never any question of any one of them remaining with me,' he informed her coldly. 'I certainly

don't expect you to have the first idea about how this
consortium runs—and I don't simply mean the London
offices, I mean the whole shebang worldwide; but that's
what I've been spending the past two years familiarising
myself with. I don't just look around the companies, or
the various sections of the larger ones. Where feasible,
and where the executives concerned are in agreement, I
actually go in and run the particular section myself for
a short period. That's the only way to gain in-depth
knowledge of what's involved. And when I do that it's
only logical that I should borrow the secretary to the
chief executive of the particular area concerned.'

'Oh—I see,' murmured Lucy with venomous
sweetness. 'I'd better put all those gossip-mongers
straight by pointing out to them that all those secretaries
they claim you've wined and dined out of office hours
were working overtime to bring you up to date with your
own business—and it was only coincidental that they
happened to be the most attractive of the bunch.' She
glanced across at him smugly, only to find his attention
had yet again strayed to the nearby table. 'Mark, why
don't you simply draw up a chair and join them?' she
hissed viciously. 'I'm sure her companion won't object
when you explain that all you're interested in is familiarising yourself with wherever it is she works!'

The instant her words were out his eyes met hers, their
goading mockery telling her he had been flirting for no
other reason than to see how, if at all, she would react—
and she had reacted all right, she accused herself angrily.

'You sound almost jealous, sweetheart,' he drawled,
obviously determined to rub as much salt as he could
into her wound.

'I've told you not to call me sweetheart,' she snapped in a vain attempt to divert to him some of her fury with herself for having fallen so easily into his trap.

'So you did—but you don't deny you were jealous,' he murmured mockingly. 'Tell me, Lucy, isn't it about time you were thinking of finding some poor unfortunate to settle down with?'

'Perhaps you'd like me to draw up a list so that you can have them thoroughly vetted,' she retorted hotly. 'I mean, that's what you'd do, isn't it?'

'But of course,' he agreed, startling her with a smile. 'I couldn't just hand you over to any Tom, Dick or Harry, now could I? Or George, Fred or Henry, for that matter.'

'Your stepbrother!' gasped Sarah Mitson from where she sat curled up in an armchair in Lucy's flat that evening.

'That's what I've just said,' snapped Lucy, feeling drained and miserable and not in the least up to the detailed explanations she knew Sarah was determined to drag from her. 'My mother's married to his father.'

'Heck, Lucy, to think you've had the droolingly delicious Mark Waterford as a stepbrother and never breathed a word of it to me—to anyone!'

'Sarah—please,' begged Lucy wearily. 'Just let me do my explaining and stop interrupting, will you?'

Sarah managed to keep her interruptions down to a few tuts and gasps for far longer than either of them would have thought possible, but eventually she broke.

'Hang on a minute, Lucy,' she begged. 'That's some accident—how exactly *did* you manage to set the school on fire?'

'It wasn't the actual school,' muttered Lucy. 'It's a bit difficult to explain, but the back of the stage in the school hall was in an old wing—part of the original building going way back. It was like a junk room with old scenery from plays and moth-eaten theatrical costumes that no one had got around to throwing out littering the place. Everyone swore that wing was haunted and the reason it was such a mess was that even the staff were too scared to give it a thorough clearing out.'

'Did you believe it was haunted?'

Lucy shrugged. 'I told the other girls I didn't, though I wish to goodness I never had,' she sighed. 'I got myself involved in a ridiculous bet with a couple of them which ended up in my agreeing to do a tour of the place…after midnight and by candle-light.'

'You must have been out of your mind,' gasped Sarah.

'I almost was by the time I'd been in there a couple of minutes,' shivered Lucy. 'I'd taken two candles, just in case one blew out…I honestly can't remember clearly what happened, except that I tripped over something and set a paper screen on fire. I was busily trying to put it out when one of the hampers of clothes next to me just went up—I don't know whether I dropped the other candle into it, or what…luckily the alarm system went off.'

'How did Mark Waterford react when you eventually explained?' asked Sarah, her look tentative.

'He didn't—because I didn't,' muttered Lucy, all this dredging up of the past making her feel wretched and depressed.

'You certainly seem to have had a screwball relationship with him—that's for sure,' observed Sarah diffidently, plainly thrown by that disclosure.

Screwball was one word for it, reflected Lucy bitterly. From the start she and Mark had always seemed to bring out the worst in one another—though, as he had been the adult and she the virtual child, surely it had been up to him to attempt rectifying that, she reasoned defensively. Yet as she continued with her story, she noted with growing discomfort, and not a little resentment, how unusually pensive her normally ebullient friend was becoming.

'That's one of the reasons I've never been able to tell any of my friends.' Lucy broke off, then added despondently, 'I knew no one would understand. And you don't—I can tell from your face, Sarah!'

'But I am trying to,' protested Sarah. 'Most kids of that age get into scrapes and rebel against the figure of authority in their lives, but I can't help feeling a bit sorry for your stepbrother, being left on the receiving end of it all. If I'd been him I'd have been fuming to have had the stroppy daughter of my father's new wife suddenly dumped on me.'

'You make it sound as though they boarded me out with him,' protested Lucy. 'I was at boarding-school to begin with—he was only there as a name for the authorities to contact if anything went wrong.'

'And I can imagine just how much you'd resent that,' murmured Sarah wryly, 'and how you'd plot to cross him whenever the opportunity arose.'

'Perhaps some of the minor scrapes I got into were simply to rile Mark,' Lucy admitted with a sigh. This

was the second time today she was finding herself seeing
the past from Mark's viewpoint, and she wasn't enjoying it in the least. 'But I had absolutely no control
over the really major incidents—I swear it!'

'You mean there were other things—apart from the
fire?'

'One or two things,' muttered Lucy uncomfortably.
'Well—only two major ones . . . and as the last only happened a couple of years ago, it shouldn't have affected
Mark in the least—but, needless to say, it did, in a
roundabout way, though I only discovered that today.'

She told Sarah about the American she had met
through a vague acquaintance and the nightmarish results of her accepting a lunch invitation from him simply
out of compassion for his apparent loneliness in a strange
city.

'I suppose I should be thankful for small mercies in
that it was only the American Press that got hold of my
name,' finished off Lucy despondently. 'Though heaven
alone knows how they managed to make the connection
between me and the Waterfords.'

'The other disaster you mentioned,' murmured Sarah,
shaking her head in sympathetic disbelief, 'surely it
wasn't on that scale?'

Lucy shrugged. 'It depends how you view my writing
off Mark's car—actually, it was by no means written
off, though it might just as well have been the way he
carried on—and still does to this day...I'm glad someone
finds this amusing,' she exclaimed indignantly, as Sarah
became convulsed with laughter.

'I'm sorry,' choked Sarah, trying desperately to control herself. 'Lucy—you did have a driving licence, didn't you?' she gasped in sudden sobering horror.

'I didn't—I was only sixteen. Though I'd had a few driving lessons in the States,' replied Lucy. 'But at the time it seemed like a life and death situation,' she sighed. 'It happened during that couple of weeks I had to stay at Mark's flat. I'd gone down to the garage—one of those massive underground places—to get something I'd left in his car, when I saw Perry, the spaniel belonging to a delightfully daffy old neighbour of Mark's. Perry was lying beside one of the bays and at first I was convinced he was dead, but he started this awful twitching when I touched him.'

'Oh, Lucy, how ghastly,' exclaimed Sarah, not in the least put out to discover this life and death emergency featured a dog rather than a human.

'It was,' agreed Lucy. 'And I was terrified the old dear would come looking for him—she absolutely worshipped him and rarely let him out of her sight. Mark had gone off with one of his women in her car—she was one I particularly loathed,' she interposed venomously, 'and I'd no idea when they'd be back. I knew there was a vet not too far away, down a side-street, which meant I wouldn't touch a main road . . . you see, I didn't want to risk carrying Perry there, in case I did further damage— at that point I was sure he'd been hit by one of the cars.'

'So you decided to take your stepbrother's car,' sighed Sarah.

Lucy nodded. 'I was perfectly aware of how wrong it was,' she admitted, 'but it somehow seemed less wrong than letting that little dog die. I managed to get him into the car without heaving him around too much and started it up with no trouble. I had learned how to reverse—but not in a car like Mark's. I'd also never come across anything like power steering before, so when I yanked the steering-wheel round I used far too much force and smashed the side of the car into one of the concrete pillars. Needless to say, I panicked and did far more damage than an experienced driver would have,' she added with a sigh.

'What about Perry?' demanded Sarah, plainly not in the least concerned about the car.

'His recovery was nothing short of miraculous,' she replied wryly. 'He was suddenly up on his feet and wagging his tail as normal. In fact, it was just then that his owner came looking for him, so I opened a window and he leapt out and bounded over to her as right as rain.'

'You're kidding!' gasped Sarah.

'It seems Perry was prone to occasional fits,' sighed Lucy, 'and it was in the tail-end of one that I found him.'

'Oh, heck,' groaned Sarah.

'Oh, heck, yes,' agreed Lucy. 'Because it was just as Perry and his mistress trotted off that Mark and his woman appeared.'

'And our Lucy, needless to say, offered no word in her own defence.' Sarah gave an exasperated shake of her head.

'I didn't get a chance, the way he started ranting at me,' protested Lucy. 'It was bad enough listening to the racket he was making, without having that smirking female witnessing it all!'

'Poor Lucy,' sighed Sarah. 'And with your track record anyway, I can't say I blame you for not bothering.' She uncurled her legs and got to her feet. 'Come on, I'll make us some tea—you deserve one after relating all that.'

As they pottered around the tiny kitchen, Lucy tried to clear her head of the oppressive gloom now clouding it.

'Sarah, I've decided I've really got to get myself organised with my writing,' she blurted out.

Sarah turned from the tray she was preparing with a look of surprise. 'I've been telling you that for months now,' she said. 'Heavens, Lucy, you've practically made it already. I thought your problem was money, but it obviously isn't. If I were you I'd pack in the job—you could go and stay with your mother and stepfather and do your writing in the lap of luxury.'

'My problem *is* money,' replied Lucy in ominously quiet tones. 'It's my mother who married into wealth, not me!'

Sarah gave her a startled look. 'But surely there's nothing to stop you staying with your own mother while you write?'

'You mean stay with my mother and sponge off the Waterfords,' exclaimed Lucy bitterly. 'One of the reasons I'm so desperate to make a financial success of my writing is that I want to be free of the Waterfords and their damned empire. It's bad enough being employed by them as some sort of poor relation, but my writing's one area where I intend succeeding without a penny of their support.'

'Lucy, I got the impression you were rather fond of your stepfather!' exclaimed Sarah in shocked tones.

'I am—I'm very fond of him,' protested Lucy, picking up the tray and taking it into the living-room. 'And I'm beginning to wish Mark had never told me about this operation coming up,' she exclaimed as she placed the tray on the coffee-table. 'What if I really *am* jinxed and get involved in something ghastly before he's recovered?'

'Don't be so silly,' said Sarah, flashing her a look of exasperation as she began pouring the tea. 'From that tirade you just delivered in the kitchen, I can only conclude it's your dishy stepbrother you want all this freedom from,' she stated, handing Lucy a cup.

'Why does everyone always have to refer to his looks?' demanded Lucy despairingly.

'Because he's an exceptionally good-looking man,' retorted Sarah sharply. 'And I must say, it makes a pleasant change to hear all the women making such openly sexist remarks about a man's looks, instead of the other way round.'

'They wouldn't drool quite so much if they knew what an overbearing tyrant he really is,' muttered Lucy. 'One of the reasons I can behave like a moron with such ease is that I spent most of my teenage years listening to him telling me I am one.'

'Oh, my poor Lucy,' groaned Sarah. 'I'd always suspected you had some sort of a hang-up about your lack of qualifications—but I'd have thought the way your writing's been received would have boosted your confidence no end on that score.'

'Sarah, they're only children's stories——'

'What do you mean, "only"?' cut in Sarah incredulously. 'They're fantastic! And the kids must have enjoyed them, otherwise the publisher wouldn't be nagging you for more. I know people with a string of degrees behind them who'd give their right arm to get into print.'

Lucy gave her a sheepish smile. She was secretly enormously proud of her small success—and it had boosted her confidence no end.

'I take it your stepbrother knows nothing of what you've achieved?' said Sarah, her expression resigned.

'You're the only person I've told,' admitted Lucy cagily.

'You've not even told your mother?'

Lucy shook her head, her feelings of discomfiture bordering on guilt as she did so.

'I want to make sure it's something I actually can do as a career before I started broadcasting it,' she said. 'And I honestly do intend getting myself organised to write more regularly,' she insisted, brightening visibly with the prospect.

'You'll make a most successful career out of it—that's for sure,' Sarah informed her confidently. 'But something tells me that all the success in the world with your writing isn't going to help cure the problem you have with the divine—in looks, that is—Mark.'

CHAPTER THREE

'YOU said you wouldn't go too fast,' complained Lucy, and was surprised when Mark instantly complied by slowing down the rate of his dictation—but only to a rate that enabled her to get down every third instead of every fifth word he uttered.

Up until now he had simply given her the gist of his letters, leaving the actual wording up to her, and it had worked well. In fact, being Mark's secretary hadn't been the trauma she had worked herself up into believing it would be—but only because he had been in his office so rarely.

'Just a little slower,' she pleaded, though in her heart of hearts she knew she should be asking him to stop altogether—her shorthand was useless!

'Hell, Lucy, if I go much slower I'll lose track of what I'm saying,' he exclaimed, scowling across the desk at her. 'Now—where was I?'

Lucy waited with growing despondency for him to continue.

'I asked you where I'd got to,' he stated impatiently. 'You'd better read it back to me.'

She gazed down at the jumble of hieroglyphics staring back at her from the pad on her knee and experienced a moment of total panic.

'I . . . I can barely read a word of it.'

'Lucy, I'm not in the mood for your juvenile humour—read the darned thing back!'

'I've told you—I can't!' she protested. 'I warned you I'd be rusty...but even I hadn't expected it to be this bad. I've just about forgotten all of it.'

'Then what the hell were you scribbling away at while I was dictating?' he demanded, leaning forwards across the desk in a manner she found more than a little intimidating.

'I was trying to take it down...but I've done it so badly I can't read it back.'

'So, might I ask what would have happened if I'd not asked you to read those few words back to me?' he demanded grimly. 'The first few words, I should point out, of what would have amounted to several pages. I suppose you'd have been quite content to let me carry on—while you continued scribbling down gibberish!'

'I've really no idea what I'd have done.' And that was the plain truth, she thought unhappily.

'So—what do we do now?'

Lucy hesitated—now was the time to tell him to stop playing around and find himself a proper secretary. 'You could use a dictating machine,' she heard herself say instead, as it suddenly occurred to her just how badly she had been handling the whole question.

As usual whenever Mark arrived on the scene, her self-confidence had deserted her. But she wasn't a halfwit, so why on earth was she confirming his low opinion of her abilities by behaving as though she were? By no means all secretaries used shorthand and there was absolutely no reason whatever why she shouldn't perform the job well once she set her mind to it.

'A dictating machine,' he murmured, as though turning the idea over in his mind. 'I could dictate into it for hours at a stretch...then you could erase the whole lot in as many seconds.'

'Despite what you may think, Mark, I'm not a congenital idiot,' she informed him sharply.

'You're wrong to think that's an idea I've ever entertained about you, sweetheart,' he drawled. 'I know darned well that any such mishap certainly wouldn't be a mistake on your part.'

'OK,' she conceded without umbrage—it was pointless denying there hadn't been times when she wouldn't have thought twice about such sabotage. 'If I promise faithfully not to erase anything...will you use one?'

'It doesn't look as though I have any choice,' he said, then promptly gave her one of those beatific smiles she had learned of old not to trust. 'And I'm so pleased you've decided to stop frothing at the mouth whenever I forget and refer to you as sweetheart...it's just one of those cosy endearments of mine that are liable to slip out from time to time.'

Cosy endearments, my foot, thought Lucy indignantly, and as for one slipping out, she doubted if anything had ever passed his lips that hadn't first been scrutinised thoroughly by that coldly calculating brain of his.

'Of course it is,' she murmured, a smile to equal his plastering itself across her face as she rose to her feet, 'so don't you give it another thought, sweetie pie.'

His eyes widened slightly, but there was amusement lurking at the corners of his mouth.

'Where do you think you're going?' he enquired.

'To find you a dictating machine.'

'Well, you don't need to look far,' he informed her, also rising, 'there's one in your office—the previous two secretaries I borrowed didn't do shorthand.'

Lucy let out a groan of pure frustration. 'Do you mean to tell me you put me through all that just for the heck of it?' she demanded angrily.

'Darling, I couldn't resist it—you know how dictatorial I am. And besides, shorthand was part of that exclusive training you had.'

'Exclusive, my eye!' exploded Lucy, his not so subtle reminder of how much her unsuccessful education had cost his father affecting her like a red rag to a bull. 'The only thing exclusive about it was the ludicrous fees they charged! The same with those ghastly crammers you kept packing me off to. All they——'

'Can it, Lucy,' he drawled, walking past her and towards her office. 'How about you rustling me up some coffee while I dig out this machine?'

Lucy hesitated, then followed him into her office. 'Yes, sweetie pie,' she murmured, chalking it up against the 'darling' he had slipped in earlier.

This time there was no hint of humour in the set of his mouth as he turned and glared at her before walking over to her desk.

Lucy busied herself with the coffee.

'What's all this?' he demanded.

Lucy spun round and found him frowning down at the draft specification on her desk.

'One of the survey teams needs it in a bit of a rush,' she said then, thrown by the expression on his face, added, 'They're used to me doing them, and, anyway, it's not as though I've been worked to death since coming up here—you're hardy ever around.'

'Well, I shall be around from now on—so they'll just have to get it done through the proper channels. And while you're telling them, I'd be grateful if you'd refresh their minds as to what those channels are. From now on you work for me and no one else—understood?'

Lucy looked at him in amazement. 'I've finished it, actually. I was just going to send the disks down for printing.'

'OK—send them down,' he growled, opening one of the cupboards behind her desk and removing a dictaphone from it.

'Mark . . . why are you so annoyed?' she asked, curiosity overcoming her.

He placed the machine on the desk, his expression slightly startled.

'Lucy, you don't seem to realise . . .' He broke off, plainly rethinking what he had been about to say. 'I've been borrowing other people's secretaries for so long— so let's just say I've become a little possessive now that I've got one of my very own.'

'Ha, ha.' Did he honestly think she would swallow rubbish like that?

'Lucy, stop trying to be cynical,' he admonished with surprising lightness. 'And try getting it into your head that you are *exactly* what I need right now and that I'm not going to stand for anyone else poaching you . . . Isn't that coffee ready yet?'

She flounced over to the percolator, her mind being tugged in different directions. Suddenly it was very important to her to do this job, not well, but brilliantly—

if only to dumbfound him. But it was he who was managing to dumbfound her right at this very moment—not that she believed a word he was saying.

'You've always made it perfectly plain that you've needed me like a hole in the head,' she accused. The old Mark was bad enough, but this somehow different version was far worse. 'So what's changed?'

'A lot,' he replied, giving her one of those smiles she so distrusted as she handed him his coffee. 'I've toured my empire and dutifully served my apprenticeships with all the experts and their super-efficient secretaries. And now that's all behind me I'll be able to get down to projects of my own in areas where I'm regarded as the expert.'

Lucy was racking her brain to remember what his particular field was. She knew he'd originally got a First in modern languages, but also that he'd immediately followed that with something else—architecture or something related to it, but she couldn't be sure.

'Didn't you mention something about those other experts having super-efficient secretaries?' she asked.

'I did, but you're missing the point. The last thing I want around me is a secretary someone else has moulded to super-efficiency. What I want——'

'What you want, in other words, is a moron like me!' exploded Lucy. She should have seen something like that coming, she remonstrated furiously with herself as she glanced down at the mug in her hand and comtemplated slinging its contents over him.

'I wouldn't if I were you,' he warned, one hand imprisoning her wrist while the other removed the mug from her grasp.

'Well, you're not me, sweetie pie...and I would have!'

'And you can stop calling me sweetie pie,' he muttered, suddenly yanking her towards him.

'Just try and stop me!'

He stopped her with ease, his mouth covering hers with a leisurely, probing kiss that blasted all coherent thought from her mind with the violence of the jolts of excitement it sent jarring through her.

She was vaguely aware that she was doing all the wrong things—such as not tearing herself free. But tearing free was the last consideration on her mind as she felt the probing heat of his mouth on hers slacken suddenly—she wanted more.

'Lucy, you know perfectly well I've work to do,' he muttered thickly against her mouth. 'And I'll insist on your making up for all this time you're wasting,' he joked weakly, then returned his attention to kissing her even more thoroughly while raising her imprisoned hand till it curved against his neck, where it was instantly joined by her other without the slightest prompting from him.

'You said you'd overstepped the line the last time you did this,' she declared in a breathily distorted voice a few moments later. 'And I'm sure this is a clear-cut case of sexual harassment.'

'You'd better report me to your union, then,' he whispered huskily.

His arms tightened and suddenly she was afraid: not of the desire manifesting itself with such blatant potency in the lean, muscled body against which hers was now trapped, but of the terrible hunger that evidence of arousal had woken in her own body.

'No!' she cried out, a softly despairing protest that it should be in these arms that her body was responding with such frightening intensity.

He released her instantly, moving away from her towards the window and standing before it with his back to her.

'There are two ways of dealing with this,' he stated tonelessly. 'We either let it run its course, or nip it here and now in the bud.'

Lucy flopped down on the chair beside her as her legs began giving way beneath her. There was little point hoping that she might have misinterpreted those coldly matter-of-fact words . . . but she hoped anyway.

'What do you mean—let it run its course?' she asked tentatively.

'For heaven's sake, Lucy, at your age that's not the sort of thing you should need spelling out,' he exclaimed impatiently. 'The last thing I expected was that you and I would start finding one another physically attractive— and it's a complication I need like a hole in the head right now.'

'You . . . you arrogant pig!' she spluttered, almost beside herself with rage.

'Call me all the names you like, Lucy, but it doesn't alter the facts,' he drawled, turning and walking back towards the desk. 'And as we're more usually at one another's throats instead of——'

'What on earth makes you think I'd even contemplate an affair with someone like you?' she cut in angrily. 'And don't start denying that was one of the options you just offered!'

'I wouldn't dream of denying it,' he replied, his eyes sweeping over her in a way that indicated he was having second thoughts about finding her even remotely attractive. 'Just as I wouldn't, if I were you, dream of denying that an affair was a decided option with someone I'd responded to in the way you have to me ... not once, but twice now.'

While Lucy floundered for the non-existent words that would crush his smug arrogance as they deftly eluded her, he picked up the machine from her desk and began walking towards the door of his own office.

'Anyway, the choice is all yours,' he stated, his back towards her. 'But I should point out that you'll not have your mother to run to if you opt for letting things take their own course and find you can't handle it—she'll have enough worries with my father for the next couple of months.' He turned as he opened the door. 'The rest of this equipment is in the cupboard behind you—make sure you familiarise yourself with it.'

Lucy gave a dazed shake of her head as the door closed behind him. This was just another example of the tortuous one-upmanship he had always practised against her, she told herself angrily. And if she had had her wits about her she would have called his bluff the instant he made his preposterous suggestion!

The work itself turned out to be varied and absorbing, and Lucy found herself, more often than not, enjoying it immensely—in fact, the only negative aspect of it was that it was Mark she was doing it for.

She sorted through what she had done that morning with a confidence she had lacked in those initial days.

Those first days had been absolute hell, she remembered with a small shudder. But he had learned not to stand over her and harry her when he wanted something done urgently—just as she had learned to rely on her not-too-reliable memory less and make notes of the rapid-fire mish-mash of instructions he would sometimes issue before disappearing. And though there were times when their tempers would flare, on the whole he left her to use her own initiative in far more areas than she would have expected.

'Did you book that table for me at the Savoy Grill?' he asked, popping his head round the door.

Lucy clapped her hand to her head. It was an instruction he had issued in the lift that morning and she had forgotten to make a note of it!

'Forget it,' he snapped. 'I'll do it myself!'

As the door slammed behind him, Lucy gritted her teeth and got on with her work. Any reasonable boss would at least wait until they were actually in the office before bombarding his secretary with instructions, she told herself indignantly... but since when could Mark ever be described as reasonable?

'Come in,' she called as she heard a knock on the outer door of her office.

'I was looking for Mark Waterford.'

The tall, expensively dressed woman who uttered those words glided towards Lucy's desk in a cloud of exotic scent.

'Is... is he expecting you?' stammered Lucy as she racked her brains to put a name to that now-familiar and, close up, stunningly beautiful face.

The woman nodded, her magnificent brown eyes cool as they flickered over Lucy. 'We're lunching together, but I'm a little early.'

'I'll just give him a buzz and let him know you're here,' said Lucy as the exotic visitor moved languidly towards the door of Mark's office.

'Don't bother—I'll tell him myself,' stated the woman imperiously. 'I take it this is his office?' Without waiting for a reply, she opened the door and glided through. 'I ran out of ways of wasting time, darling—so here I am,' she was murmuring as she closed the door behind her.

'And let's just hope darling's managed to book you both a table,' muttered Lucy under her breath, irritated by the sugary note that had entered the woman's voice the moment she had addressed Mark—she loathed women like that!

She was still trying to put a name to the woman's decidedly familiar face when Mark entered her office, still in the process of getting into his overcoat.

'There are a few things on the Spanish project on this,' he announced, handing her a tape.

Lucy glanced up as she took it, her eyes widening, not so much because the still unnamed woman was at his side and turning down the collar of his coat with fussingly proprietorial hands, but rather because of the faint smear of lipstick on Mark's mouth.

'I'll need to talk to you in detail about Spain this afternoon,' he said, while Lucy maliciously wondered if pointing out lipstick on her boss's face would be considered part of a good secretary's duties.

'I hope it won't be this afternoon, darling,' protested his companion with a throaty chuckle, tucking her arm purposefully through his, 'because I've got an idea I think you'll find much more exciting.'

Lucy remained motionless and seething at her desk as the door closed behind them. Mark's women had always fallen into two categories, as far as she was concerned—those she disliked and those she loathed. The ones she disliked were those who tried to patronise her; the others, just like the ghastly creature whose scent still hung cloyingly in the air, barely acknowledged her existence!

There was a thought lurking in the back of her mind which she was only too happy to cast aside when Sarah burst in, her expression one of amazement.

'Is it my imagination, or did I just step out of the lift to find our lord and master awaiting it—with Andrea Stuart draped all over him?'

'Andrea who?'

'Stuart,' replied Sarah, giving her a puzzled look. 'You must know her—she was in that mini-series we were discussing the other day.'

'I thought the face was familiar,' muttered Lucy. 'I was trying to think of her name—but it obviously hadn't registered with me anyway.'

'So—what was she like?'

'I thought you were supposed to be madly disapproving of people who went around ogling celebrities.'

'For heaven's sake, Lucy, what's got into you?' protested Sarah, flopping down on the nearest chair and regarding her grim-faced friend with complete bemusement. 'All I asked was what she was like. I assume you were introduced?'

'Well, I wasn't,' snapped Lucy then, shocked by the sound of her own tone, added contritely, 'I'm sorry,

Sarah, but you've just happened to catch me in an off moment.'

'I see,' murmured Sarah drolly. 'She was that ghastly, was she?'

Lucy gave a wan smile. 'Pretty much. She swanned in here like Lady Muck, then virtually straight out again with Mark in tow.' She gave a small shrug, then rose. 'Come on, let's eat—I'm starving.'

'I'm starving too,' complained Sarah as they closed the office door behind them. 'But, unlike you, I can't wolf away to my heart's content—I'd weigh a ton if I did.'

'Something tells me I'm about to be subjected to yet another of your interminable lectures on how I should do more with my appearance,' chuckled Lucy, eyeing her friend's tall, willowy figure as they entered the lift. Though not conventionally beautiful, Sarah's were the sort of looks that inevitably turned heads and there was rarely a lock of her ruler-straight, shoulder-length blonde hair out of place.

'You can stop grinning away to yourself like that,' warned Sarah. 'I happen to stick pins into your effigy each morning as I slave away for hours before a mirror— knowing that you'll waltz in without so much as a lick of make-up on you and still managing to look a million dollars.'

'If I look that good, why are you so determined to change me?' teased Lucy.

'Because, with a little help from me, you infuriating idiot, we could have you looking two or three million dollars.'

'I suppose you then plan auctioning me to the highest bidder,' murmured Lucy as they entered the elegant, wood-panelled canteen that would put many an exclusive directors' dining-room to shame.

'Anyway, I've come to a decision,' announced Sarah, as they seated themselves with their meals. 'I'm doing you over for the staff Christmas bash.'

'I beg your pardon?' choked Lucy.

'You heard,' retorted Sarah. 'I nearly died of embarrassment the way you turned up last year—you hadn't made the slightest effort whatsoever!'

'Sarah, I was flying off to the Seychelles at the crack of dawn the next morning,' protested Lucy. 'And anyway, I had bought something really special to wear.' She broke off as Sarah turned her eyes upwards in a look of long-suffering forbearance. 'The thing just dissolved on me when I tried to run an iron over it... in fact, the iron was ruined too.'

'I don't wish to hear any more,' stated Sarah primly, then immediately burst out laughing. 'But your mention of the Seychelles reminds me,' she continued when she had recovered. 'Will you be going back there again this Christmas?'

Lucy shook her head. 'Apart from the fact that there's my stepfather's operation looming up—and I'm sure they'd prefer a quiet time on their own—I simply can't afford it.'

Sarah frowned. 'With all that Waterford wealth knocking around, I'm surprised to hear that comes into it.'

Lucy felt her cheeks redden; her stepfather was the most generous of men and she would hate to give any impression to the contrary.

'It's my choice—not my stepfather's,' she said quietly. 'If I need money for fares—or for anything, in fact—all I have to do is contact the accounts department and they arrange it. But ever since I've been earning my own living I've had a thing about paying my own way.'

'But it wasn't just Christmas last year,' pointed out Sarah. 'You also went a few months earlier when your mother broke her leg ... surely you didn't fork out for that, too?'

Lucy shrugged, puzzled as to why she should suddenly feel so defensive about it. 'Sarah, it's just the way I am—and anyway, I had the royalties from my stories to help.'

'That reminds me—how's the writing going?'

'Not too brilliantly,' sighed Lucy, 'I just haven't had the time recently.'

'Lucy, you've *got* to find the time,' exclaimed Sarah in desperation. 'Do you think I haven't seen the dive your confidence has taken of late? That wretched stepbrother of yours has somehow managed to blind you to the fact that you're a talented and intelligent person—with looks most would kill for. It will do your self-confidence the world of good once your writing really takes off—which I know it will. That's why you've got to keep at it.' She threw her hands up in a gesture of disbelief. 'What really upsets me is the idea of your even needing something like that to boost you when you're such a fabulous person just as you are!'

'My, that was a speech and a half,' said Lucy unsteadily, deeply moved by her friend's undoubted sincerity.

'I suppose it was,' agreed Sarah, somewhat bashfully, then cleared the tension from the air by adding flippantly, 'Perhaps I should take it up as a career.'

CHAPTER FOUR

'ABOUT this Spanish project,' stated Mark the following morning when Lucy entered his office. 'You've seen all the suggestions—so, what do you think about it all?'

Lucy, who had been racking her brains for a suitably barbed remark concerning his failure to return to the office the previous afternoon, found herself stunned to silence by the sheer unexpectedness of his question. Was he seriously asking *her* opinion?

'Pull up a chair,' he muttered, leaning back in his own, 'and give me your honest opinion.'

Lucy sat down, her mind racing back over all the information it had absorbed on the subject.

'Well—for a start I'd reject all those plans entailing the demolition of all those citrus groves...it would seem such a shame.' She gave him a furtive look to gauge his reaction and found, to her amazement, that he was nodding in agreement.

'The only problem is that we're contractually bound to come up with some sort of development that attracts income to the area and also creates a measure of local employment,' stated Mark, a brooding look on his face as he pinched his bottom lip between his thumb and forefinger.

'It's not clear to me why Waterford's bought the land in the first place,' admitted Lucy, disturbed to find her mind unaccountably filling with pictures of Andrea Stuart clinging to his arm.

'It was just one of those odds and ends that came with the Iberian Group when we bought them up,' replied Mark. 'Unfortunately the finer points of Spanish law weren't brought sufficiently to our attention at the time, not that it would have affected our bid in the least. But it seems we have to submit plans to the local authority by early spring, otherwise we come up against all sorts of penalties.' He straightened and gave her a sudden grin. 'There's something I find rather quixotic about the whole thing—which is why I've decided to run the project myself.'

Lucy's eyes widened in surprise; there were far more prestigious schemes in the Waterford's pipeline, any one of which she would have felt more likely to appeal to him than one tucked away in southern Spain.

'Which plan have you decided to use?'

'I'm not sure I'll use any of them,' he replied with a shrug. 'I got into conversation a few days ago with a most interesting character—a retired professor of agronomics from around that region. He gave me one or two things to think about, which is why I've decided to go there after Christmas and have a good look round for myself.'

'I suppose that means you won't be needing all that bumf I've churned out for the files,' Lucy almost groaned, remembering all the hours of work it had entailed, then made a mental note to remember to look up 'agronomics' in the dictionary.

'We might as well play it safe and take those files with us,' he chuckled. 'You never know, we might need to extrapolate one or two things from them.'

Lucy nodded, slightly thrown by the 'we' until it occurred to her that he would probably be taking a survey team with him.

'Any comment?' he asked, something in his tone triggering off a vague bell of alarm in her.

'Nothing I can think of,' she replied warily, while silently berating herself for being so ridiculously jittery. 'Would you like some coffee?'

'My, but you are turning into the perfect little secretary,' he drawled, his tone setting up a clanging of alarm bells within her. 'Soon I'll be wondering what I ever did without you.'

'Which only goes to prove that I'm not quite the moron you've always taken me for,' snapped Lucy, now fully on her guard.

'Lucy, I can't imagine where you get the idea that I take you for a moron,' he stated with no discernible sincerity, rising and stretching lazily.

'You amaze me,' she retorted, eyeing him warily as he began walking around the desk to her side of it.

'I'm sure not half as much as you do me at times,' he murmured, coming to a halt behind her and placing his hands on her shoulders. 'And what amazes me most of all is the inordinate length of time it apparently can take you to come to relatively simple decisions.'

Lucy ducked free of his hands, leaping to her feet and rounding on him angrily.

'Whatever it is you're complaining about, I'll have you know that for the past few weeks I've tried in every way I can to learn how to be a good secretary. Unlike a lot of people taking over a job like this, I haven't had the luxury of a predecessor to overlap with. I realise I've made mistakes, but, instead of giving me any credit for what little I have achieved, all you can come up with is sarcastically veiled references to my alleged inability to make decisions that I wasn't aware I was supposed to be making in the first place!'

'If there's a wrong end of a stick to be grasped, you can be relied on to grasp it,' he exclaimed in disbelief. 'I'm fully prepared to give you credit for the way you've tackled the job—though why I should, when it's exactly as I expected you to, is debatable.'

'Exactly as you expected?' Lucy was irritated to hear the words come out as an inane croak.

'Precisely. Though that's not what we're discussing right now,' he snapped. 'Some time ago I asked you to come to a decision about our—for want of a better word—relationship. I'm still waiting.'

Lucy leaned back weakly against the desk—this was one line of goading she had become lulled into believing he had discarded.

'How remiss of me,' she retorted in a fair imitation of his own drawl. 'I'd decided some time ago that it might be rather interesting to have a brief relationship—for want of a better word,' she mimicked sweetly, 'with someone the antithesis of all that appeals to me in a man. Unfortunately, yesterday afternoon reminded me of the sort of creatures you get involved with and I realised I couldn't stomach the idea of being lumped together with them.'

As she was speaking she found herself unable to drag her eyes away from the series of expressions flitting so rapidly across his handsome features that it was impossible to catch and identify a single one. But it was a look of cynical amusement that finally, and rather disappointingly, she found, settled on his face. That look remained there as he lifted aside the chair impeding his access to her and stepped forward, his body trapping hers against the desk.

'Mark, you——'

'So,' he cut imperiously across her words, 'I'm the antithesis of all that appeals to you in a man, am I?'

She nodded vigorously, not trusting herself to speak. But she resisted with all her strength when he reached out and took her into his arms.

'The trouble is, I don't believe you any more than you appear to believe me,' he taunted softly, his arms trapping her to stillness. 'And, unlike you, I can probably prove I wasn't lying.'

'You either can or you can't,' she snapped, hating him for the aching throb of need his touch had already awakened in her, and for his coldly manipulative exploitation of his ability to create such a need.

'OK—I'm certain I can,' he whispered, his mouth taking hers with a bruising hunger.

Her response to the violence of the passion with which he laid siege to her senses was recklessly uninhibited and without a shred of thought of any consequences. As though possessed of a will of its own, her body arched to his, melting ardently to the searing heat it encountered, while her hands roamed in restless, hesitant impatience against him. At first she tried removing his jacket from him, but got no assistance from the arms tightening even closer around her. Then her trembling fingers began loosening his tie, impatiently abandoning that idea and simply opting for undoing the buttons of his shirt. He responded instantly, a shudder jarring through him, while his arm tightened almost to a point of suffocation around her, making further movement an impossibility.

'No!' he groaned, biting passionately against her mouth.

She began to shake her head in protest against the restraining fierceness of his hold, then felt the sensuous movement of his hips against hers and the instant, rhythmic response of her own body.

'No!' This time his denial was accompanied by the sudden stilling of his body against hers and he let out an incoherent groan as he wrenched himself completely free of her. 'Lucy, I swear it was never my intention to prove my point quite as forcefully as that,' he whispered, his words ragged and unsteady as he stood with his back to her. 'But there's no denying I proved it.'

'Oh, no, there's no denying that!' exclaimed Lucy, the words exploding in breathless bitterness from her. Even she had never dreamed he could stoop this low! 'And what am I supposed to do now? Say, "Yes, Mark, any time you feel like an affair, I'm available," so that you can fall about the place laughing at the very idea?'

He spun round, his tie askew, his shirt half-undone and his face dark with fury.

'My God, I might just as well address you in Greek for all the difference it would make!' he bellowed furiously. 'Do I really have to spell it out in words of one

syllable? I wasn't trying to prove that you respond physically to me, damn it—I was simply trying to get it into
your thick skull that I respond to you equally disastrously, and I do mean disastrously!'

'Mark, stop shouting,' she pleaded weakly, her head
reeling.

'I'm shouting because it seems to be the only way I
can get through to you,' he roared. 'And you can forget
about making decisions because I'm making them—and
we're putting a halt to this as of now!' He dragged his
fingers through his hair, shaking his head as he glared
at her in disbelief. 'And to think I was actually worried
about how this might affect you,' he exclaimed. 'I'd have
ended up certifiable within a week!'

'You actually would have given it a whole week, would
you?' murmured Lucy, feeling suddenly extraordinarily
light-headed.

'Probably not,' he scowled, 'but that's something we'll
never find out, thank God.'

'Why this sudden change of mind?' she enquired,
realising that, in all the years she had known him, this
was the first time she had ever experienced having the
upper hand... and it was the most exhilarating of
sensations.

'It's more a return to my senses than a change of
mind,' he muttered, returning to his side of the desk,
his expression disgruntled as he flung himself down on
the chair.

Lucy also sat down, her innate wariness where this
man was concerned already beginning to temper her
elation as she waited for him to continue.

'Though I might have worded it more charitably than you did, your reference to the sort of women who usually attract me was undoubtedly a pertinent one,' he stated, tilting his head back against the dark leather of the headrest and closing his eyes in contemplation. 'In fact, you were probably stating no more than the truth when you said I'm the opposite of what normally attracts you in a man,' he continued.

Lucy wondered if it was her imagination that his tone seemed to imply that only a severe flaw in her basic character could account for such an aberration. But as her eyes took their leisurely stock of him, she discovered that the sight of his still thoroughly dishevelled appearance was starting up an aching sensation in the pit of her stomach which was disconcertingly like hunger. Yes, there was a terrible flaw in her make-up, a fatalistic voice from within informed her with chilling candour, because Mark Waterford had always been, still was and probably always would be, the epitome of all she had ever wanted in a man... which was tantamount to admitting she was some sort of emotional freak, she concluded despairingly.

'Lucy, I find myself dredging the depths of my mind for anything that might explain this ludicrous turn of events...perhaps the mere fact of living out of a suitcase, at least mentally if not in physical actuality, has disorientated me.' He shifted restlessly in the chair, his eyes opening to flicker accusingly towards hers, then instantly away. 'Hell, there has to be some explanation other than my having turned into a raving lunatic!'

The implication being that only a raving lunatic would find her desirable, Lucy informed herself, almost boiling with rage. And what incensed her beyond reason was that he seemed to imply that her finding him equally desirable was no more than was to be expected!

'For all I know, you *are* a raving lunatic!' she exploded, then immediately tried to calm herself; if she wasn't careful, she could come out of this ghastly exchange with her pride in tatters. 'But as for me—at least there are extenuating circumstances to account for my behaving so profoundly out of character,' she exclaimed less heatedly, while frantically racking her brain for the details he would undoubtedly demand in an instant. 'I...I've just ended a long relationship with a man I love deeply,' she fabricated off the cuff. 'And who loves me deeply,' she added, just to make doubly sure he was getting the intended message.

'With all this depth of love knocking around, it seems a waste to end it,' he drawled sceptically, though there was a sudden sharpness in his eyes.

'I...he wanted to get married,' improvised Lucy, a voice inside her shrieking out a warning not to tie herself up in knots. 'I wasn't ready for marriage just yet.'

He leaned across the desk on his elbows, his eyes narrowed and astute as they watched her.

'And how long did this—deeply loving—relationship last?'

'Two years...well, almost.'

'Two years—and you still don't feel ready for marriage to this man you love so deeply,' he murmured, his brows arching in mocking question.

Lucy clamped her lips tightly shut. All right, so she had overdone the 'deeply,' she told herself irritably, but if she lost her temper now she wouldn't stand a chance.

'And how is all this meant to explain away the un-bounded enthusiasm with which you responded to me?' he demanded silkily. 'It's the last way I'd have expected a woman in love with another man to react.'

It was then that it all came flooding back to her exactly why she had to be so completely on her guard—and why, years ago, she had given up trying to lie her way out of tight corners with Mark. He had always caught her out—and with humiliating ease. But not this time, she prayed silently; this time her pride would never survive it.

'I . . . we had an intensely physical relationship,' she muttered then, desperate to counteract those weakly stammered words, added defiantly, 'I can assure you that it came as a decidedly unpleasant shock to find myself responding to you at all, let alone as reflexly as I did.'

'Reflexly?' he enquired, that single ungrammatical word oozing venom.

'As I told you, it was an intensely physical relation-ship,' she replied, the pleasure she gained from wit-nessing the look of undisguised fury with which he greeted those words going a little way towards lessening her own shock at actually having mouthed them.

'With reflexes such as you're claiming,' he stated in glacial tones, 'it looks as though some young Spaniard or other is in for the time of his life.'

'Spaniard?' croaked Lucy, then felt herself grow cold as the full impact of his insult hit her.

'Who else would you expect to populate Spain?' he enquired coldly. 'Danes—or Russians, perhaps?'

'Are you saying I'm expected to accompany you to Spain?' she gasped, realising even as she did so that she had misinterpreted precisely that earlier.

'Are you trying to be funny?' he snapped, his patience plainly wearing dangerously thin.

'No. It's just that, when you said "we", I thought you meant you and a survey team,' she protested. And that was the story of their lives, she told herself bitterly; he came out with obscure pronouncements and she was always too tied up in knots ever to question them.

'I'll be dealing with any surveying needed at this stage—ably assisted by my competent secretary.'

Lucy's eyes dropped from the drill-like coldness of his to rest on the hands clenched tightly on her lap as she weighed up the likely consequences of an outright refusal.

'Though, if you feel you might not be able to trust yourself with me...' He rounded off his unfinished words with the most eloquent of shrugs.

'I'm hardly likely to pounce on you, for heaven's sake!' exploded Lucy, instantly casting aside all thought of refusing to go. 'And as you've promised not to——'

'Promised?' he cut in, wide-eyed with mocking innocence. 'I've promised nothing. All I've said is that I want this whole ridiculous thing to stop. But, having gone against every instinct I possess in letting it start in the first place, there's no guarantee that I won't lapse again...especially if we find ourselves holed up in the back of beyond with no other distractions.'

'If that's the case, I suggest you bring one of your numerous female distractions along with you!' Lucy almost screeched at him as she leapt to her feet in fury. 'You might have caught me off guard once, but try it again and it could end up the last mistake you ever make!'

'What would you do, darling?' he drawled, his lips twitching with amusement. 'Love me to death? And as for catching you off guard—once, yes; twice, I suppose there's room for you being given the benefit of the doubt—but *three* times?'

'Sarah, there's no point spending hours putting my hair up,' groaned Lucy, twisting impatiently on the dressing table stool. 'By the time we get there it'll be straggling all over the place and a complete mess.'

'Lucy, just sit still and shut up, will you?' admonished Sarah amiably, deftly catching up the blonde swath of Lucy's hair and twisting it high on her head. 'There,' she exclaimed with satisfaction moments later. 'Up in seconds, totally secure and utterly fabulous.'

'How would I know?' complained Lucy, glancing with exasperation at the towel draped over the mirror before her. 'You'll have to let me see what you've done to me at some point—and I warn you, if I don't like it I'm not going.'

'Has anyone ever told you what an ungrateful brat you can be at times?' murmured Sarah with a chuckle, then tutted as she looked at her watch. 'Actually, we'd better get a move on, the taxi will be here any minute now.' She flicked her fingers deftly through Lucy's hair. 'How does it feel?'

Lucy gave her head a tentative shake, then another more vigorous one.

'Heavens, what have you done?' she exclaimed. 'Welded it up?'

'Just a couple of tortoiseshell pins—which I'll kill you if you lose—and a bit of know-how. So... are you ready for the unveiling?' she chuckled, reaching over and whipping away the towel with a flourish. 'Well?' she demanded anxiously, as Lucy made no sound.

'It...it's not me,' stammered Lucy, after several further seconds' inspection of the ethereal creature staring back at her from the mirror. 'How on earth did you get my hair looking so soft and natural? It always looks tortuously scraped back whenever I try doing it like that.'

'That's because you're not the genius I am,' murmured Sarah modestly. 'Now—stand up and let's see the rest of you.'

Lucy stood up, turning towards the mirrored wardrobe door and gazing in bemusement at the stranger in the deceptively simple navy silk shift dress, the tie shoulders of which Sarah was now adjusting.

'You know, I wasn't too sure about this dress when I saw it on the hanger,' admitted Sarah, stepping back to examine her handywork, 'but it looks sensational on— very understated, yet decidedly sexy...I bet it cost a fortune.'

Lucy's heart sank, not so much because the dress actually had cost her far more than she could really afford, but because Sarah was right about how it looked. It was the simplest of dresses, no more than a V-necked tube of soft silk to be stepped into and casually tied at each shoulder, yet it managed to skim lightly against each curve of her slim body with a voluptuousness not apparent when she had tried it on.

'If I were holding my breath to hear your verdict, I'd be unconscious by now,' exclaimed Sarah. 'So tell me for heaven's sake—do you approve?'

As Lucy took yet another look in the mirror, the subtly yet dramatically emphasised eyes before her widened in disbelieving unison with her own.

'You've done a fantastic job,' she croaked, then added with a wail, 'but it isn't me, Sarah! I'm going to feel like some kid at a party in her mother's make-up—and that's how everyone else is going to see me!'

'What you really mean is that you're worried that's how big brother is going to see you,' said Sarah with an exasperated sigh. 'Well, I can guarantee his eyes will be out on stalks just the same as those of all the other guys at this do—otherwise he's not the man he's reputed to be.'

'And what, exactly, is he reputed to be?' asked Lucy, caught completely off guard.

'You're obviously not aware that his so-called relationship with Andrea Stuart has been plastered all over the gossip columns of late,' chuckled Sarah.

'No, I'm not. And anyway, what's so-called about his relationship with her?' she asked, attempting a tone of bored disdain.

Sarah's reply was a yelp of consternation. 'Heck, there's the taxi! And I've been so busy getting you all dolled up, I probably look a wreck myself,' she accused as they grabbed their bags and coats and dashed out to the waiting cab.

'Sarah, you look fabulous,' Lucy laughingly informed her immaculately groomed friend as the cab sped them away. 'So stop fishing for compliments.'

'So—where was I?' grinned Sarah, supremely confident as ever, then pursed her lips primly. 'Or was I boring you with all that gossip?'

Lucy flashed her a look of impatience.

'OK,' chuckled Sarah. 'They're all oozing tongue-in-cheek sympathy for the gorgeous Andrea—I get the impression she's not the most popular of stars with the Press. They're all revelling in our lord and master's notoriety as a heart-breaker. According to them, it's common knowledge that his trail is littered left, right and centre with broken-hearted beauties. You wouldn't believe some of the names they've named!'

'We should have brought an umbrella,' muttered Lucy, feeling nothing but gratitude for the rain suddenly bucketing down from the night skies.

Sarah gave her a startled look, but said nothing.

'And I can't think why I let myself allow you to talk me into coming to this wretched do in the first place,' continued Lucy morosely, too preoccupied by the gloom that had descended on her to realise how odd her sudden and manic darting from topic to topic was sounding.

'Lucy, love, everyone comes to the staff Christmas do, no matter what—you included,' pointed out Sarah quietly. 'Why should this year suddenly be so different?'

'Why indeed?' said Lucy and was horrified by the stark despair in her tone.

'Oh, Lucy, what on earth am I going to do about you?' groaned Sarah, reaching out and unexpectedly giving her hand a sympathetic squeeze. 'You and that wretched stepbrother of yours,' she sighed, shaking her head. 'It's impossible to tell whether you're frightened of him, in awe of him or just plain in love with him—it's a relationship that's not in the least healthy; in fact, it verges on being downright kinky!' She broke off with a groan of contrition. 'When will I ever learn to keep my big mouth shut?'

'Poor Sarah,' murmured Lucy, laughing despite herself. 'I suppose my feelings towards Mark could be any one or all three of your suggestions—though,' she added despondently, 'if I ever decide I'm in love with him, it would be your duty as a friend to have me certified.'

'Perhaps I'm the one you should be having certified,' groaned Sarah, gazing miserably out of the rain-splattered window as the cab drew up outside the famous hotel at which the Waterford staff Christmas parties were traditionally held. 'I've been dolling you up to the nines to make sure he notices you're a big girl now, but that's something I should be thinking twice about doing even to my worse enemy, judging by how he's reputed to treat big girls.'

As she paid the taxi driver, Lucy was wondering how Sarah would react to hearing that Mark had already noticed she was no longer a child...and how disastrously she had handled it. Sarah was worried enough as it was, she decided grimly.

'How civilised,' murmured Sarah as a uniformed commissionaire, holding a huge umbrella aloft, opened the cab door. 'Talk about a lamb being led to the slaughter,' she added gloomily.

'Don't be too sure about that,' said Lucy, catching a sudden glimpse of her own reflection in the huge plate glass doors being held open for them and feeling her spirits unaccountably soar.

'What are you up to?' demanded Sarah, managing to look both anxious and suspicious at the same time.

'It might be a little early for New Year resolutions, but I've decided it's about time I really grew up.'

And another thing she had decided was that, just because her feelings towards Mark had always been a jumble of confusion, there was no reason to compound that confusion by entertaining the ludicrous idea of being in love with him. And as for his branding himself a raving lunatic for finding her physically attractive, which he unquestionably did, she reminded herself with an unsuppressible shiver of excitement—tonight she would show him just how many raving lunatics there were around.

CHAPTER FIVE

'LUCY, don't you think you're asking for trouble?' nagged Sarah out of the corner of her mouth. 'He's hardly taken his eyes off you for the past hour or so. For heaven's sake, he is your boss—you can't keep on avoiding him like this.'

'Want to bet?' asked Lucy, laughing as she was dragged off towards the dance-floor by yet another of their throng of male admirers.

'I've always said you were one of the best lookers in Waterford's,' murmured her partner amorously against her hair. 'But tonight you're sensational, Lucy...I'm lost for words.'

'Yet you've just managed quite a mouthful of them, Jim,' replied Lucy drily.

She was beginning to feel sick and tired of all these fulsome references to her looks. Bar the lick of paint and the flattering dress, she thought indignantly, she was the same person she had always been. Though she had always had more than she could handle of male attention before, she was finding this concentrated blast of it oddly depressing—it was all so shallow.

'Sorry to butt in, you two,' apologised a girl with a familiar face to which Lucy was unable to put a name, 'but Mr Waterford says he needs to speak to you, Lucy.'

'Has Mr Waterford lost the use of his legs or something?' demanded Lucy, then was immediately contrite—it wasn't his poor messenger's fault. 'Sorry,' she muttered, both to her partner, from whose reluctant arms she disengaged herself, and the startled-looking girl. 'It's probably something rather urgent.' Like hell it would be, she thought angrily, having to force a smile to her lips as the girl began accompanying her. 'It's OK, I can find my way over to him; you go off and enjoy yourself— you don't want to leave yourself open to being used as a messenger all night.'

She weaved her way through the mass of people towards where Mark stood in scowling isolation by the archway leading into the buffet hall, conscious of his hooded eyes monitoring her every step. This time she was going to remain cool and calm, she chanted to herself as she made her slow progress; this time she wasn't going to let him tie her up in a single knot.

'I thought you were supposed to be my secretary,' were his coldly accusing words of greeting when she eventually reached him.

'So did I,' she replied unconcernedly, still inwardly chanting her vows.

He flashed her a blackly scowling look. 'Then why aren't you behaving as though you were?'

'Because, believe it or not, Mark,' she replied, steeling herself to remain composed, 'I don't regard being your secretary as a lifetime vocation. It's a job I carry out between certain hours, and right now doesn't fall into that period.'

'This is a business function,' he growled. 'And it also happens to be the first such a one I've attended in London—I expected you at my side to show me the ropes.'

'Show *you* the ropes?' she chuckled in genuine amusement. 'Mark, if you need me to show you how to mingle with your employees and enjoy yourself——' Her words gasped to a halt as he grabbed her by the arms and yanked her towards him. 'Mark, are you out of your mind?' she groaned, her vow swept from her mind by the frantic prayer that the floor would open up and swallow them both.

'Don't tell me the fact we have an audience disturbs you,' he taunted, anger glittering in his eyes.

Lucy clamped her lips tightly shut, her new-found confidence deserting her as she fatalistically accepted that an audience, no matter what its size or composition, would be the last thing he would be disturbed by.

'All right,' she capitulated, her teeth clenched, 'if you need to be led by the hand and shown how to mingle, let's get on with it.'

'That won't be necessary,' he murmured, his expression one of almost gloating satisfaction as he released her.

'So why the hell was I summoned over here?' demanded Lucy, the last vestiges of her composure now gone.

'I was jealous, darling,' he drawled, his eyes openly predatory as they swept over her. 'I'm not used to being cold-shouldered by the belle of the ball.'

'I hate you,' spat Lucy, a measure of her confidence unexpectedly restored with the realisation that she had spoken only the truth. 'You've just got your own way by threatening to create a scene ... that's blackmail and you're despicable!'

'I suppose I am rather,' he agreed blandly. 'But now that I've succeeded in getting my own way—let's dance.'

'Dance?' she almost shrieked, then hastily lowered her voice several decibels. 'You mean to tell me you had me summoned over here for you to tell me you wanted to dance with me?'

'Sorry to disappoint you, darling, but no,' he informed her in bored tones. 'It's just that I learned a few hours ago that I'm needed at the New York office. As I'll be leaving first thing in the morning, there are obviously several things we'll need to discuss.' He reached out and took her chin in his hand, tilting her head up towards his still disconcertingly predatory gaze. 'And, as a concession to your troublesome paranoia regarding business hours, I thought you would feel less of the downtrodden slave you so obviously regard yourself as were we to dance as we talked—though naturally you're free to claim overtime for this inhumane encroachment into your pathetically few hours of hard-earned liberty.'

'I think it could be said you've made your point,' muttered Lucy, her head threatening to swim with all the words bombarding it.

'I'm glad to hear it,' he replied, a glimmer of amusement softening his features. 'I was worried in case I might have left out something pertinent,' he added with a chuckle, then took her hand and led her imperiously towards the dance-floor, seemingly oblivious of the heads swivelling in their direction.

Of course all eyes would be on them, decided Lucy angrily, refusing to be lulled by his unexpected flash of humour. He hadn't danced with a single other woman all evening and she wouldn't put it past him to have not done so deliberately, simply in order to make an embarrassingly ostentatious exception of her.

'You're holding me too tightly,' she whispered fiercely as he swept her into his arms and lowered his cheek to hers.

'Am I?' he whispered seductively, his words a tingling breath against her ear. 'Are you cold, Lucy? You're shivering.'

She was; but it wasn't shivering so much as a trembling that blanketed and smothered to oblivion all the resolve that had earlier so fired her. How could she possibly feel like this in the arms of someone she claimed to hate—someone she so often *did* hate with a blinding intensity? Sarah was right, it was downright kinky, she told herself miserably... but admitting it didn't alter anything.

'Right—are you listening carefully?' he asked in those same seductive tones, and proceeded to bombard her with a list of instructions to be carried out in his absence.

He knew how he was affecting her, she told herself with angry resentment as she strove to take in something of what he was saying while at the same time trying to curb the demented racing of her pulses—he knew, and yet he seemed to get some sort of perverted pleasure from doing so! It was just as she sensed her anger was beginning to prevail over the effect he was having on her senses that his arms shifted slightly around her. It was no more than the most minimal of movements, yet it was one that brought her body into contact with the beat of his heart. The heavy thud she encountered might not have been racing quite as chaotically as her own, but it was most definitely racing, and the knowledge that it was filled her with a giddy sensation of exhilaration.

'Now repeat that back to me,' he whispered, his hands moving against her back, leaving heat still tingling where they had been and creating more where they now alighted. He leaned back slightly to gaze down at her from darkened, sultry eyes. 'Well?'

'How can I?' she murmured, that giddy sense of exhilaration still holding her in its thrall making her oblivious of the bodies around them as she gazed almost flirtatiously up into the luminous darkness of his eyes. 'You know I've a memory like a sieve if I don't take notes.'

'Do I?' he asked, his eyes narrowing slightly.

'You should do by now,' she said, her voice suddenly faltering and uncertain as the bubble within her seemed to burst.

'Perhaps my mind is temporarily clouded by the fact that I have the belle of the ball in my arms.'

'What is it with you?' she demanded, his drawling coldness dashing to nothing what little remained of her giddy exhilaration. 'Even at a party, where all those around you are enjoying themselves, you still have to resort to your usual sneering sarcasm!'

'Sometimes there's a danger in enjoying oneself too much,' he said, his hand sliding up her back to clasp at the nape of her neck, making movement of her head virtually impossible.

'There's a fat chance of that with you around,' she retorted with undisguised bitterness, loathing herself for having become so ridiculously carried away by the fact that her nearness had excited him. He had already made it perfectly plain that he found her physically attractive, she reminded herself angrily, just as he had also made it even plainer that he regarded it as something of an unfortunate joke.

'Are you saying you weren't enjoying yourself?' he whispered, his arms tightening and returning their bodies to suffocating closeness.

'Mark, stop it!' The harshness in her tone was in complete contradiction to the acquiescent softness with which her body was yielding to his.

'Perhaps your problem—one of your many, I might add—is that you don't find being the belle of the ball all it's cracked up to be,' he mocked softly against her hair as he drew her head down against him.

'As usual, I've no idea what you're talking about,' she muttered, trying desperately to restrain her body from answering the seductive call of his and wondering how on earth his body was capable of imparting messages of such languid sensuality while his words coldly mocked.

'Haven't you?' he taunted. 'You've had men buzzing around you all night, like bees to the proverbial honey-pot; but what I find so intriguing is your apparent distaste for it.'

'What makes you think I find it distasteful?' Although discomfited by his perception, she wasn't prepared to admit it as such.

'Like most of the other men here, I've hardly had my eyes off you all night.'

'If that's the case, it only goes to show you're as shallow and short-sighted as the rest of them,' she retorted, angered and thoroughly confused by his behaviour.

'I can assure you, darling, my eyesight's perfect,' he murmured complacently.

'You know damn well what I mean!' she exclaimed heatedly, then made a concerted effort to regain control of herself as she remembered where they were. 'Just because I let Sarah talk me into letting her slap a bit of paint on me, it doesn't turn me into someone else! Yet suddenly men I've known for ages are slavering over me as though I'm the last female left on the planet. I'm still the same me, for heaven's sake! Men like that make me sick!'

'You'd better come down from your cloud, Lucy,' he informed her harshly, drawing her head back from him till she was looking up into the cold blue of his eyes. 'Because that's the way it is. And I can assure you that women are the culprits every bit as much as the men,' he added with a venomous disgust that startled her.

'Not the sort of men I respect,' she retorted, but her mind was elsewhere, the unguarded venom in his tone triggering memories in her of how women had always reacted to his extraordinarily good looks.

'How remiss of me to overlook your deeply loving paragon of virtue,' he muttered coldly, suddenly jerking her so close to him that she almost tripped over his feet. 'The one you love so deeply in return, yet not, apparently, sufficiently deeply to marry him.'

'I wouldn't even attempt to explain,' she retorted airily, her irritation over his biting sarcasm overridden by gratitude; her phantom lover had almost slipped her mind, 'because I doubt if you'd be capable of understanding what constitutes decency in a man.'

'Well, if it's not slavering over you in your warpaint that constitutes it, then I'm afraid you'll have to admit I qualify,' he murmured, his eyes glittering ice as his body burned in sultry heat against hers, 'because I'd already started slavering long before your friend got to work on you with her paintbox.'

'Except that you also informed me of your opinion that only a raving lunatic could find me attractive,' Lucy lashed out, almost beside herself with fury.

'And my, how that rankles,' he taunted, clamping his cheek once again against hers. 'Tell me, Lucy, is that why you decided to try your hand at dazzling me tonight?'

'My God, how conceited can you get?' she gasped, doggedly refusing to acknowledge just how close to the truth his taunting words had been. 'You must be completely out of your mind,' she added for good measure.

'Must I?' he laughed, then suddenly began spinning their bodies with dizzying abandon.

'Mark, stop it,' she begged, clinging on to him for dear life as they careered into another couple and she began losing her footing.

He spun them to a halt, calling out words of apology to the couple they had bumped into and laughing down into Lucy's outraged face.

'What on earth did you think you were doing?' she exclaimed angrily. 'You could have . . .' The words faded on her lips as she saw the laughter die on his face and become replaced by an expression she found it impossible to interpret.

'I could have what?' he whispered slightly unsteadily, his eyes burning down into hers.

She tried to speak, but all that emerged was a stifled gasp.

'Lucy?' he whispered hoarsely, his head lowering with painstaking slowness towards hers. 'Damn you,' he breathed, then jerked back his head as though only then regaining control of it, his expression harshening. 'You're treading on very dangerous ground with me, Lucy—but I wonder if you realise exactly how dangerous.'

Of course she did, she thought numbly, still shaken by how dangerously close he had come to kissing her...and by the inescapable fact that she wouldn't have put up the slightest resistance if he had.

'Why the hell didn't you do the normal thing and marry lover-boy?' he demanded angrily, seemingly oblivious of the fact that they were now standing stock-still in a mass of dancing couples. 'Forget I ever asked that,' he sighed, his arms dropping from around her. 'Since when have you ever been known to do anything even remotely resembling normal?' He took her by the arm. 'Come on, let's get some food—I'm hungry.'

Lucy followed his ducking and weaving steps until they reached the room where the buffet was being served, so lost in her own tortuous thoughts that she was cut off from all awareness of her surroundings.

There was barely a single coherent thought in her head, she remonstrated wearily within herself—and this time, just this once, she had intended it to be so different.

'Would you like something to eat?' asked Mark, his tone verging on impatience as she stood behind him, lost in her own world of self-recrimination.

Lucy nodded vaguely, her mind battling to unravel all those knots into which it had been so deftly tied.

Several moments later, when he handed her a plate of food, she glanced down at it and then up at him, a puzzled frown on her face.

'Thanks ... but you didn't have to get it for me,' she muttered.

'You showed no signs of getting it for yourself,' he snapped. 'We'd better grab one of those tables—I can't abide eating standing up.'

Lucy followed him over to one of the few empty tables, placing the plate he had handed her down on it.

'What time do these functions normally end?' he demanded, drawing out a chair for her to sit on.

'I've no idea,' replied Lucy, striving not to be further unsettled by his cool urbanity. 'Though I'm sure it's some time well past midnight,' she added.

He glanced down at his watch, pulled a face and began eating.

Lucy waited for him to say more, then gave an irritable shrug and began picking with little interest at the food before her. If it was such a chore for him being here, she thought angrily, why the hell had he bothered coming?

'I'm sure no one will mind in the least if you leave,' she informed him baldly.

'Not even you, darling?' he murmured with a cynical smile.

'Especially not me,' she retorted. 'In fact, I can't wait for you to go so that I can relax and start enjoying myself.'

'What—with one of those shallow, short-sighted men who so sicken you?'

'I didn't say they were all like that,' she muttered, picking up a fork and stabbing it viciously into the food.

'Perhaps not,' he drawled, 'but I'm sorry to hear that relaxing and enjoying yourself is something you find so difficult with me around.'

'Difficult?' she demanded contemptuously. 'With you around I find most things difficult—if not impossible! Most of the time I'm hard-pressed simply trying to keep my wits about me!'

'My, that's some effect I have on you,' he mocked, 'but, if it's any consolation, the feeling's quite mutual.'

'You know damned well what I mean,' exploded Lucy. 'Ever since I was a child you've played cat and mouse with me; either tearing strips off me for my alleged crimes and telling me what a moron I am or shrivelling me with your sarcasm—and nothing's changed!'

'Correction—some things haven't changed,' he snarled, slamming down his knife and fork and angrily pushing aside his plate. 'You're still the petulant, spoiled brat you always were—and the only thing that's changed there is that nowadays you come more attractively packaged!'

'Packaged?' squeaked Lucy, almost beside herself with rage. 'That's exactly how you see women, isn't it? Pretty little packages for you to unwrap and enjoy for a while, then cast aside!'

And the most horrifying thing about it, she suddenly saw, was his ability to keep his mind so coldly apart from his body's seductive pursuits. No wonder she had been reduced to total confusion tonight, she thought bitterly, when the potent messages with which his body had bombarded her had been so completely at odds with those of his aloofly mocking mind.

'Which only goes to show that whatever it is I'm looking for, I've yet to find,' he replied, a curious flatness in his words.

'I suppose it depends on what you're looking for,' muttered Lucy, wary at having been let off so lightly and unconsciously bracing herself for his delayed retaliation.

'Isn't it supposed to be love that we're all searching for so manically?' he demanded harshly. 'Though apparently not you, Lucy... Or did this deep love you claim to have found fail to live up to your expectations?'

'All I said was that I wasn't ready for marriage,' she protested weakly, wondering for how long he would go on dredging up that one lie she was beginning to regret she had ever uttered.

'If it meant that much to him and you love him as much as you claim, you'd have married him ... at least, that's my opinion—for what it's worth.'

'And how much is it worth?' demanded Lucy scathingly. 'Exactly what do you know about love?'

'Not ever having found myself in that unfortunate state—nothing.'

'Yet you still seem to feel qualified to accuse me of being abnormal for not marrying someone I say I love.'

'Lucy, as I've always said, I might as well address you in Greek for all the difference it would make,' he exclaimed impatiently, frowning as he seemed to gaze into the distance behind her. 'I expressed a wish that you'd married this apparently nameless paragon—but for purely selfish reasons.'

'So that you can be relieved of your role of big brother—is that it?' she demanded angrily and instantly regretted those rash words as he began laughing with derisory softness.

'I'd have thought that by now even you would have got it into your head that brotherliness has no bearing on my feelings towards you,' he murmured mockingly. 'What I was trying to convey to you was that I regard married women as strictly off limits—that's all.' He reached across the table and took one of her hands in his. 'Lucy, why don't you do us all a favour,' he murmured in tones that were close to being seductive, 'lover-boy included—and marry him?'

For an instant she gazed across at him in disbelieving horror, then quickly snatched her hand away.

'You're unbelievable—and you're also sick!' she protested hoarsely.

'And you're kidding yourself, darling,' he drawled, his eyes once again glancing past her. 'Perhaps not about me, but certainly about being in love... Can't you see how much safer you'd have been in anyone else's hands but mine?'

'I thought it was your avowed intention to keep your hands to yourself where I'm concerned,' she accused frigidly, while heat blazed on her cheeks.

'Oh, but it is,' he murmured urbanely, his eyes flickering lazily to her mouth before meeting hers. 'But, being a realistic man, I accept that there has to be a limit to the extent of my will-power.' He shook his head as she made to remonstrate furiously with him. 'Lucy, I'm not trying to be clever or sarcastic or anything else—I'm merely stating the facts. And they're facts that, if you're honest, you'll admit apply equally to us both.'

She opened her mouth to deny that claim, then snapped it shut with a sigh. She gazed across the table in silent pleading and was answered with a brief shrug of his shoulders and a grin that was boyishly wry and which startled her profoundly.

'This is crazy,' she groaned involuntarily. 'Mark, I . . . do I really have to go to Spain with you?'

Yet again he seemed to glance over her shoulder, then leaned back on his chair, frowning.

'Don't think I haven't thought about that,' he muttered, 'but yes, you do. We can be charitable, if you like, and describe you as disaster-prone; but while Dad's recuperating I'm not prepared to take any risks—I want you right where I can monitor exactly what you're up to and, if necessary, avert any trouble you're likely to get yourself into.'

'For heaven's sake, how many times do I——?'

'Before you start frothing at the mouth yet again,' he interrupted coldly, all trace of that brief moment of boyish diffidence gone from him, 'I should warn you that your artistic friend is finally about to join us. She's been dithering around for some time trying to make up her mind whether to. Now that she has, we should make an effort to make her feel welcome, wouldn't you agree?'

He rose to his feet as Lucy twisted round on her chair and saw an unusually diffident-looking Sarah approaching.

'Lucy and I were about to have coffee—will you join us?' Mark murmured politely.

'Oh, thanks…I'd love to,' stammered Sarah, watching wide-eyed as he fetched her a chair from a nearby table, then picked up the two barely touched plates and strode off with them.

'Heck, he really is divine,' Sarah drooled, her eyes still on that tall departing figure as she sat down. 'I've been dithering around for ages, wondering if you needed rescuing,' she exclaimed accusingly, turning her attention to her grim-faced companion. 'On the other hand, I was loath to interrupt if things were going all right.'

'I can assure you, things never go all right between Mark and me,' replied Lucy wearily, feeling suddenly utterly drained. 'In fact, you came just in time to avert the umpteenth row we've had tonight.'

'I must say I thought the pair of you looked a little fraught from what I could see of you just now,' sighed Sarah, then added with a chuckle, 'though rowing's not the word I or anyone else here would have used to describe the way the two of you seemed to be inter-relating on the dance-floor.'

'For heaven's sake, Sarah,' began Lucy, then clamped her mouth tightly shut as Mark returned with a tray, which he placed on the table before returning to his seat.

'Don't tell me I'm supposed to pour as well as fetch and carry,' murmured Mark with one of his most disarming smiles.

Sarah responded with an answering smile and immediately began pouring, while Lucy glowered across the table at him.

He would be charm personified now that Sarah had joined them, she told herself bitterly, and Sarah, like every friend she had ever possessed, would succumb to that invidious charm.

'Lucy, aren't you going to introduce us?' he chided lightly.

Knowing full well he knew exactly who Sarah was, Lucy clenched her teeth and made woodenly formal introductions.

'I didn't quite catch your surname,' quipped Sarah to Mark, who repeated it with deadpan politeness at which, to Lucy's irritation, the two of them began laughing as though they had cracked the joke of the century.

'I'm sorry I had to drag Lucy away,' said Mark, once he had sufficiently composed himself, 'but I'm off to the States first thing in the morning and we had business to discuss.' As he spoke he glanced at his watch. 'I'd hate to offend anyone by leaving too early,' he sighed disarmingly, 'but I really am catching a very early flight.'

Lucy, who considered herself well-versed in his ability to offend without so much as a qualm, went rigid with disbelief.

'Heavens, I'm sure no one would mind if you slipped away,' gushed Sarah. 'And it's late anyway—lots of people have left already.' She turned to Lucy. 'In fact, I was wondering if it wasn't about time we made a move—we're going to have problems getting a cab.'

'I'm afraid you're wasting your time trying to get Lucy to leave,' murmured Mark with an air of boyish innocence. 'She's determined to stay to the bitter end.' He broke off with an indulgent chuckle that Lucy found particularly grating. 'She was just telling me that we've you to thank for her stunning appearance tonight,' he added, this time, Lucy felt, overdoing the wide-eyed innocence.

Sarah gave a slightly embarrassed little shrug, plainly completely taken in.

'Tell me, Sarah—as one of our Lucy's closest friends— would you say she was the marrying kind?'

This time even Sarah looked nonplussed, a look un- observed by Lucy, who was too preoccupied with con- templating sliding under the table.

'Of course she is!' exclaimed Sarah as she recovered her wits. 'She just hasn't met the right man yet.'

Lucy felt her cheeks flame as Mark turned to her with a look of feigned bemusement.

'Sarah only says that,' she managed from between clenched teeth, 'because she can't stand...' she froze for one terrible moment, then plucked a name from the air '...George.'

'So...far from being a paragon, George is somewhat loathsome, is he?' Mark enquired innocently of Sarah.

'Not loathsome, exactly,' replied Sarah without so much as a flicker of hesitation, 'more of a wimp—in my opinion, that is.'

'And I'm sure you're an admirable judge,' murmured Mark, chuckling as he picked up his cup and then drained it. 'Anyway, I'm afraid it's time I was off—but, if either or both of you need a lift, you're welcome to one.'

Sarah turned to Lucy with a look of pleading. 'We'll be ages getting a cab.'

Lucy gave a shrug and got to her feet.

'I suppose we could go over those things you want done while you're away,' she muttered in Mark's di- rection as he too rose.

'Good idea,' he replied. 'But perhaps we should drop Sarah off first, so as not to bore her to tears.'

'Sarah's spending the night at my place,' pointed out Lucy woodenly, the colour once again flaring in her cheeks as he gave her a look that mocked and challenged and did several other things besides.

'Perhaps that's just as well,' he murmured, deliberately pausing before adding, 'With a memory as bad as yours, Sarah's might prove a handy back-up.'

CHAPTER SIX

IT WAS at an extremely early hour in the morning of the third day of the new year that Sarah Mitson closed the front door of Lucy's flat behind them and steered her bleary-eyed friend towards the kitchen.

'Right—that's the car seen to,' she said, giving Lucy an encouraging push towards one of the two chairs on either side of the small kitchen table. 'You flop yourself down while I pour the coffee, then, if you really insist, we can go through the check-list yet again.'

Lucy, her face pinched and wan, nodded. 'I honestly don't know what I'd have done without you, Sarah.'

'Neither do I,' retorted Sarah, placing two mugs of coffee on the table before taking the other seat. 'And for heaven's sake cheer up,' she groaned. 'You're off to sunny Spain—not to mention the fact you'll be in the company of the man of most girls' dreams.'

'I thought Jonathan was supposed to be the man of your dreams,' muttered Lucy, striving without much success to look cheerful.

'He is,' chuckled Sarah. 'I was merely expressing what seems to be the opinion of the vast majority of the female population regarding Mark Waterford, that's all.'

'There's no accounting for taste,' muttered Lucy gloomily. 'And as for sunny Spain, you obviously haven't heard that they're in the throes of one of the worst winters ever known there.'

'Lucy, must we really go through all that again?' groaned Sarah exasperatedly. 'OK, the weather's lousy in Spain; Mark's plane could be delayed and you could miss the boat from Plymouth. And yes, you could have an unfortunate accident on the way to the airport and write off the second of his precious cars. And even if none of those disasters materialises, there's the possibility that he'll flip when he sees all the equipment you've loaded up the car with—not to mention——'

'I really have been a pain,' groaned Lucy as she recognised she was being quoted almost word for word. 'Sarah, I'm sorry—really I am. I honestly don't know how I've got myself into this ridiculous state.'

'Neither do I,' sighed Sarah. 'For heaven's sake, Lucy, all you've done is follow what few instructions he's given you to the best of your ability. And he's the one insisting on stepping off a plane from America and on to a boat for Spain all in one day. If anything goes wrong, it's entirely down to him. Why the man couldn't wait for the next boat is beyond me.'

'Because it means waiting another week,' Lucy pointed out half-heartedly. 'The boat only sails once a week during the winter.'

'Well, he should have made an effort to get back sooner,' retorted Sarah. 'Why should you be the one getting in such a tizz when he's the one cutting everything so fine?' She flashed Lucy a sympathetic grin. 'But just to make you feel better, we'll double, if not triple, double-check what we've just loaded into the car.'

'Oh, heck—the suitcase of his clothes I collected from his housekeeper!' squeaked Lucy.

'In the boot along with your things,' chuckled Sarah, flashing her an exasperated look. 'There's the word processor, all the feasibility study files, the——'

'Oh, forget it,' groaned Lucy wearily. 'As you say, we've already been over it more than enough times. And yes,' she added, with a sudden grin, 'the tickets, my passport and all the car documents are in my handbag.'

'My God, the girl's actually beginning to resemble a human being,' teased Sarah, rolling her eyes in disbelief.

'Thanks to that coffee,' retorted Lucy. 'This is hardly what you could call a civilised hour to be up.'

'Agreed,' chuckled Sarah. 'But you were up with the dicky birds to go walking with my father over Christmas.'

'That was different—I was enjoying myself,' protested Lucy. 'I loved our early morning walks along the front... In fact, spending Christmas and New Year with you and your parents in Brighton was sheer perfection,' she sighed wistfully.

'Personally, I felt George should have been invited along too,' murmured Sarah, struggling to keep her face straight before she finally gave in to laughter. 'Lucy, I always meant to ask—why did you pick on the name George?' she choked.

'It happened to be the first name to enter my head,' retorted Lucy, her own lips twitching while she strove to sound disapproving.

Still chuckling, Sarah glanced at her watch. 'We've time for another coffee,' she announced. 'The plane isn't due for ages yet.'

Lucy shook her head and rose. 'Sarah, I don't care if I'm there an hour early—just as long as I'm there in good time.'

Sarah rolled her eyes disbelievingly, but made no remark as she too rose.

'Lucy, stop twittering, will you?' she was exclaiming exasperatedly as the two of them made their way down to the entrance hall. 'No, I haven't lost the spare key you gave me!'

'Well, Mrs Dixon next door has another spare in case you do,' said Lucy. 'She's back from New Zealand—she rang me on her way here from her sister's yesterday. She's insisting on keeping an eye on the place for me while I'm away because I did the same for her—I've told her you'll be using it from time to time.'

'That's the second time you've told me that,' pointed out Sarah with a grin. 'Heck, Lucy, the postman won't have been yet!' she groaned as Lucy darted over to a row of post-boxes and inserted a key in one.

'But I forgot to check yesterday,' muttered Lucy, frowning as she drew out a small bundle of letters held together with a rubber band. She gave an exclamation of irritation as she read the attached note. 'It's from Mrs Dixon—it seems the postman's been putting the odd letter of mine in her box.' She flicked quickly through the bundle. 'Heck, there are a couple of birthday cards here I didn't get!'

'Your birthday was ages ago.'

'Mrs D's been away for ages,' replied Lucy. 'Four months, in fact.'

'Lucy, there's no point going through those now,' protested Sarah. 'Bung them in your bag and look at them later.'

Lucy hesitated, then placed the bundle in her bag, conscious that she was already employing delaying tactics.

'You'll freeze out here in your dressing-gown,' she chided Sarah as they stepped outside.

'I've been in and out dressed like this for the past hour,' chuckled Sarah, giving her a hug. 'And besides, it's worth it just to be able to watch you kangaroo off down the road in this classy jalopy,' she added, as Lucy climbed into the large navy BMW parked at the kerb. 'I bet you haven't the first idea what a machine like this one costs!'

'And I don't want to know,' groaned Lucy, laughing despite herself as she started up the powerful motor. 'At least it's big enough to take all this gear.'

'If you wait a mo, I'll nip up and get the kitchen sink,' offered Sarah, producing a large white handkerchief from her dressing-gown pocket and holding it theatrically to her face as Lucy rolled up the window and blew her a kiss.

It would have been fantastic if she and Sarah had been making this trip, thought Lucy wistfully, a reminiscent smile lingering on her face as she rounded the corner. Her smile faded to a look of tension as she thought of the man with whom she would be making the journey. But beneath the stomach-lurching nervousness that accompanied that thought there was an underlying *frisson* of excitement too strong to be denied and which, for one panic-stricken moment, resulted in her contemplating turning the car round and heading in any direction other than the airport.

* * *

Whereas the other passengers filtered in orderly fashion through from the customs hall, the only thing missing from Mark Waterford's entry, as far as Lucy could see, was a fanfare of trumpets.

Now what? thought Lucy nervously as she watched two stewardesses plus two airline officials, not to mention a flustered, bejewelled and befurred middle-aged woman, dance attendance around a scowling Mark's tall figure. It was only when he turned and caught sight of her that Lucy noticed his right eye; it was almost closed and a largish area around it red and ominously puffy.

With a minimal nod in Lucy's direction, he wrested the trolley containing his luggage from the official pushing it and continued towards her.

'As I've already told you, not only is there no need for all this fuss, but I've a tight schedule to keep to,' he impatiently informed his entourage.

'We'd feel a lot happier if you agreed to see a doctor,' said one of the officials anxiously.

'You might, but I wouldn't,' snapped Mark. 'I tell you, a couple of aspirins will see me fine.' He walked up to Lucy, muttering to her as he continued on past her. 'Come on, let's get out of this place.'

'And a happy New Year to you too,' muttered Lucy under her breath as she followed after him.

'So—what happened to your eye?' she eventually asked, breaking the silence he had shown no inclination to disturb on their way to the car park.

'One of my fellow passengers took it upon herself to clobber me over the head with a champagne bottle.'

'Good heavens, what did you do to her?' gasped Lucy.

He flashed her a wryly amused look. 'I'd forgotten how uncompromisingly literally you tend to take my every utterance,' he murmured. 'I didn't do anything to the wretched woman—she happened to drop the bottle on me when she was removing her mountain of hand luggage out of the overhead locker.'

Wide-eyed with alarm, Lucy grabbed him by the arm as they reached the car.

'Mark, you could be concussed, for heaven's sake!' she exclaimed. 'You were mad not to wait and see a doctor!'

'The keys,' he snapped, shrugging his arm free of her panicked hold and trying the boot.

'Mark—you've got to listen to reason!'

'Lucy, I am not concussed,' he informed her with exaggerated patience. 'And neither am I a congenital idiot. Had I felt in need of a doctor's services, I'd have waited and seen one. Now—may I have the keys?'

Not in the least reassured, Lucy reluctantly handed over the keys. The eye was now more or less completely closed and the red around it seemed to have spread and darkened almost to bruising.

'Good girl,' he drawled as he opened the boot and saw what was already stored in it. 'You actually remembered to collect my things.'

'Don't be so damned patronising,' she retorted hotly, her mind filling with vivid images of him keeling over from delayed reaction to massive brain damage.

He flashed her a scowling look, then slammed shut the boot and went to the driver's door.

'Just hang on one moment,' stated Lucy in the most forbidding tone she could muster. 'If you think I intend getting in this car with you at the wheel—think again, Mark.'

'For God's sake, Lucy, we haven't got all day—get in the damned car!'

'You're right—we haven't got all day; the boat leaves at one,' she replied evenly. 'So you'd better give me the keys if you want us to catch it.'

He hesitated, then shrugged as he handed her the keys. 'I suppose it is still the wee small hours of the morning as far as my body's concerned,' he conceded.

Almost light-headed with relief, Lucy got into the car and started it up. With a bit of luck he would sleep all the way to Plymouth, she reasoned optimistically.

They were barely free of the airport when he began trying to adjust his seat and muttering impatiently under his breath when it failed to respond.

'What the hell have you done to this seat?' he demanded accusingly.

Lucy's heart sank. 'I had to put it forward to accommodate all those files you wanted—and a few other things,' she muttered. This was all she needed, she thought nervously—and to crown it all she was having problems remembering exactly which motorway she needed to aim for.

'What other things?' he bellowed, releasing his seatbelt to give him the freedom to inspect the back of his car—the floor of which was packed with a word processor and sundry accessories. 'Lucy, what the hell *is* all that?'

'Before you start ranting and raving, I'd like to point out that I tried to contact you about it, but you were never there,' she protested angrily. She had spent hours agonising over how much to take.

'I spoke to you several times, damn it, so why didn't you consult me then?'

'Because it wasn't until later that the question of what to take in the way of equipment occurred to me...and you never rang back after that.'

'I suppose it didn't occur to you that I hadn't mentioned it simply because I didn't consider we needed any?' he enquired, re-locking his seatbelt. 'Though as I omitted to get you to check if we could hire hardware compatible with ours, I suppose it's just as well you used your initiative—even if, as it appears, you decided to include the kitchen sink.'

'Does that mean you're not going to insist it's dumped on the quayside?'

'I guess it does,' he replied, then gave a soft chuckle that sent a most disturbing shiver down the length of her spine. 'So—tell me about your Christmas. Where did you spend it?'

'In Brighton, with Sarah and her parents. It was wonderful. And yours?'

'Great.'

His tone was such that it was impossible to define it as either serious or sarcastic. Probably the former, decided Lucy wryly, remembering the surge of publicity surrounding Andrea Stuart's decision to follow him to New York.

'I tried ringing you at your flat at the New Year,' he stated later, interrupting her vain attempt to dredge up a charitable thought concerning the actress whose ostentatious posturings before the television cameras had made her blood boil at the time.

'I spent that in Brighton too. I rang my mother and your father,' she added, her tone sharpening. 'From what wasn't said, I gather they're unaware I know about his operation.'

'They still seem to regard you as a child to be protected from life's little unpleasantnesses,' he drawled. 'One wonders if they'll ever get around to accepting that you're now an adult.'

'Oh, does one?' snapped Lucy, incensed by his tone. 'And you think you're treating me like an adult by dragging me off to Spain simply to ensure I don't get into any mischief—is that it?'

'You're my secretary and I need you in Spain,' he replied, then added sarcastically, 'Anyway, you know what a cautious man I am...but not so cautious that I crawl down motorways at speeds a cyclist could better. For God's sake, Lucy, put your foot down—we're in danger of missing next week's boat at this rate!'

'I happen to be keeping to the speed limit,' she retorted defensively—in fact, she was doing so only with difficulty, never having driven a car with so immense an excess of power before.

They were on the outskirts of Plymouth before they exchanged any further words and it was Lucy who broke the silence, reddening slightly as he again caught her glancing surreptitiously at him to see if he was asleep and finding him wide awake.

'It must be my driving,' she murmured in an attempt at joking.

'What must be your driving?'

'The fact that, dog-tired though you must be, you haven't so much as once nodded off.'

He gave another of those soft chuckles that disrupted her pulse-rate, something that she again doggedly relegated to the back of her mind.

'Lucy, I've been consciously fighting sleep ever since we started off,' he admitted, 'but it's no reflection on your driving. I find the quickest way to readjust my body clock and reduce jet lag is to force myself to adhere to local time immediately.'

'Does it work?'

'Let's just say I never end up quite the state you were in that first time you arrived back from the States,' he chuckled.

Lucy gave him a startled look, then forced her eyes back to the road. It amazed her that he remembered, and even more that he had understood: she had always believed he had put her disorientated behaviour then down to deliberate wilfulness.

'How's your head?' she surprised herself by asking.

'I'm trying to ignore it,' he muttered.

'Mark, why on earth didn't you say something?' she exclaimed remorsefully. 'We could have stopped off and got you aspirins or something!'

'I'll get something once we're on board. And then you'll have your work cut out keeping me awake until bedtime.'

His subdued listlessness, coupled by the livid bruising now covering the entire area surrounding his eye, made Lucy throw caution to the winds and seek out the ship's doctor an hour after they had sailed.

'What did you do—look up just as the bottle was dropped?' asked the doctor as a surprisingly docile Mark submitted himself to his examination.

'How did you guess?' murmured Mark laconically.

'Well, I dare say you'll have a thumping head for a couple of days, but there aren't any signs of major damage,' stated the doctor as he finished an examination Lucy found comfortingly painstaking and which Mark was beginning to show signs of being irritated by. The doctor rummaged around in his bag and counted some pills into a small container. 'Take a couple of these now and get yourself off to bed,' he instructed as he scribbled something on the container. 'Then take them when necessary and according to the instructions I've jotted down.'

'As I informed them at the airport,' stated Mark frigidly, once the doctor had left the cabin, 'I'm perfectly capable of deciding whether or not I need the services of a doctor.'

Lucy, who had spent the entire time wedged against one of the cabin walls to steady herself against the increasing roll of the boat, felt her blood boil at such ingratitude.

'I couldn't, quite frankly, give a damn what happens to you under normal circumstances,' she informed him in equally frigid tones. 'But I have no intention of ending up stranded in the back of beyond with you collapsing on me simply because you're too stupid to see a doctor!'

'And to think I harboured an illusion that you were concerned about me,' he drawled, rising from the bed on which he had been seated and strolling over to gaze out of the porthole. 'We'd better get some breakfast...or

is it lunch? Whatever damned meal it is one has at this
time of day—let's get it.'

Lucy froze, her confidence in the thoroughness of the
doctor's examination faltering badly... Was he actually
beginning to ramble, or was it simply jet lag taking its
toll?

'The restaurants won't be open until dinnertime,' she
stated cautiously. 'If you like, I'll book us a table and
come and waken you in plenty of time.'

He swung round and scowled blackly at her.

'For heaven's sake, Mark, you heard what the doctor
said!'

'I heard what he said,' he retorted uncooperatively.
'And I also happen to know that if I sleep now it'll be
days before I get myself back into sync. And anyway,
I'm hungry. There's bound to be a cafeteria serving food
now—let's find it.'

He returned to the bed and picked up his jacket.

'Aren't you at least going to take a couple of those
pills the doctor gave you?' pleaded Lucy.

'I'll take them tonight—OK?'

She hesitated, then gave a resigned shrug before following him across the alarmingly heaving floor to the
door.

'And stop trying to mother me,' he admonished with
a derisory chuckle. 'I'm big enough to look after
myself—or hadn't you noticed?' He reached out, pre-
venting her falling against him as the boat suddenly
pitched steeply. 'So, you had noticed,' he murmured,
leaning slightly towards her and then, contrary to every
expectation jarring through her, righting her and releasing her.

'I do hope you're a good sailor,' he said, holding the cabin door open for her, 'because rumour has it we're in for a pretty turbulent crossing.'

To Lucy's relief, and despite the fact that others seemed to be dropping like ninepins around them, she found herself to be an exceptionally good sailor. In fact, she found the wind and the rain, lashing against her face as they braved an open deck after their evening meal, one of the most exhilarating sensations she had ever experienced.

'Lucy, I know I asked you to help keep me awake,' roared Mark over the din of the elements as they clung to one another while reeling drunkenly along the deck, 'but don't you think this is overdoing it just a tiny bit?'

'You're awake, aren't you?' she laughed, alive to the tingle of salt against her face and the fact that they were, possibly for the first time, totally at one in their enjoyment of the raging magnificence of the storm.

'As far as a half-drowned man ever could be,' he agreed laughingly, holding her tightly against him as he steered her towards a door and wrenched it open. 'Come on, enough is enough,' he said, bundling her through. 'And besides, we'll be late for the cinema.'

'The cinema?' exclaimed Lucy, lowering the hood of her drenched raincoat, then removing the coat entirely as the air-conditioned warmth enveloping her made her feel slightly claustrophobic.

'Yes, the cinema,' he reiterated, his expression amused as he too removed his raincoat. 'There's a well-reviewed thriller on—one that, with a bit of luck, should keep me from nodding off before my allotted bedtime.' He glanced down at his watch. 'In fact, it starts in a few minutes.'

'And who am I to interfere with your allotted bedtime?' teased Lucy, feeling more exhilarated and alive than she had in a long time.

'Precisely,' he chuckled, taking out his wallet. 'So, off you go and get the tickets while I dump these in one of the cabins,' he said, handing her some money and taking her raincoat from her.

Her answering smile, as she gazed up at him, faltered as he turned slightly, the brightness of the lightning suddenly accentuating the damage to his face.

'Mark, that's some shiner you've got there...' Her words trailed away as he pulled a long-suffering face. 'Well, how about if I try getting hold of a raw steak to put on it?' she tried again, the joke falling with a thud.

'And how about if you stop fussing and just get the tickets?' he suggested, grinning as he walked past her and towards the cabins.

Lucy gave a light-hearted shrug, then made her stumbling, reeling way towards the cinema deck. It was the sound of her own chuckles of enjoyment as she lurched from side to side, clutching on to whatever she could for support, that eventually brought her to a bemused halt.

Here she was, she thought dazedly, embarked on a journey she had never wanted to make in the first place and with a man she professed to loathe, on top of which they were heading towards the Bay of Biscay in a gale-force storm... and all she was doing was laughing from sheer enjoyment of it all!

She resumed her lurching journey and eventually reached the ticket desk, yet, try as she might to do something about the lunatic delight bubbling within her—it bubbled on unscathed.

She had just got round to posing herself the question of whether she would have felt quite like this if her companion had been anyone other than Mark, when he rounded the corner, his tall, lean figure coping with the treacherous roll of the boat in a way she had found impossible to master...and with him came the answer to her question.

'I bounced my way off the walls,' she greeted him, the words tumbling from her in a jerky breathlessness brought about by the fact that she was feeling exactly as she would have had someone punched her violently in the stomach.

'Did you hurt yourself?' he demanded, his expression anxious as he rushed to her side.

'No, I...' She shook her head, her words drying up on her as she frantically tried to work out what it was his appearance had triggered off in her. She cleared her throat and tried again. 'I...I'm merely green with envy that you can keep your balance so well,' she managed, handing him his change and the tickets. 'All I can do is stagger.'

He pocketed his change, his wary look warning her he wasn't fully convinced.

'But once I've managed to stagger to my seat, I bet you I'll work out who's the villain in this film before you do,' she challenged with a forced smile. 'If we ever get to see it, that is.'

'You're on,' he laughed, his expression relaxing as he gave her a mocking bow and held out his arm to her. 'So much for our fellow sailors,' he muttered as they entered the cinema and found only five other people seated. 'One of the crew mentioned that the boat was three-quarters full, yet this is the biggest crowd I've seen in the past hour or so.'

They took their seats just as the credits were coming up on the screen and all of three minutes into the film he turned to her and announced, in an embarrassingly loud stage whisper, 'I've seen it before—the vicar did it.'

'Mark!' groaned Lucy, as all but one of the five heads turned to glare in their direction.

A couple of minutes later, when one of the stars of the film appeared on screen in the role of a vicar, she turned, half laughing in exasperation, to give him a piece of her mind, only to find his body sagging towards her.

'Mark!' she exclaimed, nudging him sharply.

His response was a disgruntled repositioning of his body which resulted in his ending up sprawled halfway across her seat and with his head on her shoulder.

'Mark?'

'Mmm?'

'Are you asleep?'

'Mmm.'

'I don't mind if we skip this.' Especially not if the vicar actually had done it, she added indignantly to herself.

He stirred, easing his weight fractionally from her.

'I'm not asleep—I'm just relaxing till I get my second wind...which I shall any moment now,' he muttered irritably.

A few seconds later his head was firmly back on her shoulder and her discreet attempts to waken him brought such loud protests from him that someone actually called out in complaint.

Fuming, Lucy glared down at the glossy head nestled in such an abandonment of comfort against her, then spent the best part of half an hour trying vainly to grasp what seemed like the most tortuous of plots.

'Damn you, Mark,' she whispered savagely, wondering if it was worth risking the commotion he would be bound to make if she simply heaved him aside and left. 'Why the hell won't you wake up?' she hissed accusingly as she reluctantly decided it wasn't worth the risk. 'And if you make so much as a single snide remark about my letting you sleep, I'll...Mark?' Filled with hope as he momentarily stirred, she reached over and ruffled his hair, hope deserting her swiftly as he flung an arm out and around her and repositioned himself even more comfortably against her.

She began giggling weakly as she was forced to use her free arm to extricate her other, trapped between the armrest and his body and rapidly losing all sensation. Once it was free, she dropped it from a height around his shoulder in a last-ditch attempt at waking him. His response was little more than a minimal shift of his right shoulder which resulted in her arm falling more neatly into place around him. By this time she was almost hysterical with laughter, burying her face against his head to stifle the choking noises now emanating from her.

He smelled so good, she thought, as the giggles sub-sided in her and her pulses leapt almost lazily into an erratic, pounding beat. And he felt so good too, she ad-mitted to herself as she dreamily let her cheek rub against the silky thickness of his hair. She closed her eyes, leading her mind step by step back to that moment when he had rounded the corner. She had accepted that part—if not all—of the exhilaration she was feeling stemmed from his presence . . . but there had been something else; something much worse. Perhaps it was just the shock of facing up to the fact of just how physically attractive she found him, she reasoned half-heartedly, then gave a silent groan. It should hardly come as a shock to her now, she told herself angrily, considering the fact she had been attracted to him on and off ever since the first time she set eyes on him! Yes, she informed herself with savage cynicism, she and just about half the female population around were attracted to Mark Waterford . . . but only a complete and utter moron would allow it to go any deeper than that.

It was Mark's voice that woke her as the lights went up around them.

'A fat lot of good you'd be as a nightwatchman,' he was muttering accusingly, startling her into wakefulness as he none too gently began disentangling their entwined bodies. 'Hell, I came here with a headache and a black eye,' he continued in the same tone, 'to which I can now add a stiff neck and an arm that feels dead.'

'For heaven's sake stop whingeing!' snapped Lucy, who was never at her best when suddenly woken. 'I had people glaring at me over the racket you made when I tried to wake you—what was I supposed to do, ignore them and scream at you?'

'You could have tried something,' he growled, scowling down at her as he got to his feet, and pointedly rubbing at his neck. 'I hope you realise that the worst thing I could possibly have done was sleep for a couple of hours like that. Now I'm totally disorientated—I'll probably be awake for the rest of the night!'

'Oh, you poor darling!' snarled Lucy, lurching up from her seat. 'I suggest you get yourself a bottle of whisky or something and use it to wash down a handful of the pills the doctor gave you—the chances are you'll sleep like a baby!'

'The chances are I'd sleep forever on a concoction like that,' he growled, following after her as she reeled past the seats and into the aisle.

'Considering how paranoid you are about your wretched sleeping patterns, it's a chance I thought you'd be only too willing to take.'

'My, but we are the little shrew,' he drawled, sending her sprawling before him by walking straight into her as she stopped to counteract a juddering roll of the boat.

'I may be a shrew,' she hissed, angrily brushing aside the hand he reached out to her, 'but one thing's for sure: I'm not a complete and utter moron!'

'I don't recall calling you one,' he retorted, his look bemused.

'I didn't say you did,' she informed him haughtily as she began staggering off in completely the opposite direction to their cabins. 'I was just telling you I'm not one!'

CHAPTER SEVEN

AFTER a night spent being pitched and tossed all over the place, Lucy staggered to breakfast to find Mark already seated at the table and engrossed in the previous day's paper. Had it not been for the fact that her mind kept straying towards her stepfather and his imminent surgery, her companion's disinclination towards conversation would have suited her very well.

She suspected it was going to be one of those days that simply went from bad to worse when the boat leapt into one of its more spectacular rolls just as she was raising her cup to her lips and she found herself drenched in scalding coffee. But it was only once they were off the boat and on to the open road that her suspicion became fully compounded. It hadn't occurred to her to give a first, let alone a second, thought to what being a passenger travelling in a right-hand-drive car on Continental roads might involve—something she was finding impossible to believe, now that she was experiencing the full horrors of it first hand.

A dismal mixture of sleet and rain lashing down on roads which were ice-coated and so steep that they were like precipices, and the fact that Mark seemed determined to drive in the middle of the road, were but minor considerations once it dawned on her that they were going in completely the wrong direction. In normal circumstances she would have been quite happy to let him drive on, relishing anticipation of the moment when he would realise his mistake. But these weren't normal circumstances, and the idea of prolonging this nerve-racking journey a second longer than necessary didn't appeal to her in the least.

'Is this the scenic route or something?' she enquired with relish, determined to get a crumb of pleasure from it.

He flashed her one of those baleful looks at which he was so adept, then returned his attention to the road.

'Unless I'm very much mistaken,' she tried again, 'this is the road to Bilbao.'

'That's what all the signposts have been claiming,' he drawled.

'But Madrid's in completely the opposite direction,' she exclaimed. Any fool who had bothered to look at a map of Spain would have seen they went virtually in a straight line from the port of Santander, through Madrid and on south-east to their final destination!

'If you wanted to go via Madrid, why the hell didn't you mention it before now?' he demanded exasperatedly.

'I don't want to go via anywhere in particular,' she groaned, beginning to wish she hadn't bothered opening her mouth. 'I simply expected you to take the most direct route—— For God's sake, Mark, there's a car coming straight for me!'

'If you're going to have hysterics every time I pull out to get a better view, I suggest you bindfold yourself,' he snapped. 'And as for the route we're taking, this is the one that'll get us there quickest—hold-ups around Madrid are the norm rather than the exception.'

'How long will it take?' asked Lucy, her thoroughly deflated spirits rising marginally as he finally overtook the lorry they had been trailing for several miles.

'If we get stuck behind many more of these darned things, I'd say a week,' he growled uninformatively, swinging out and overtaking two more lorries.

'A week?' echoed Lucy weakly.

'My scintillating wit is obviously lost on you,' he murmured with a chuckle. 'Normally there would be no problem doing the journey in one haul, and I'm still hoping we can, unless this weather gets any worse.'

Lucy glanced out of the window and decided that, apart from an actual blizzard, there seemed little scope for the weather to get any worse.

She sank back against her seat, her heart in her mouth as he began overtaking a line of huge articulated lorries whose engines seemed to shriek in protest against climbing the twisting, mountainous roads before them. But once they had left the smoke-belching suburbs of Bilbao behind them, the awesome grandeur of the rain-swept scenery unfolding before her brought a lump to her throat. There was an almost brutal quality to the beauty of the vast, multicoloured mountains rearing up from stark, rain-lashed plains, with tiny, almost medieval-looking villages scattered along their bases and often clinging high up against their sides.

Feeling suddenly insignificant and almost crushed in the face of such magnificence, Lucy turned from it with an involuntary sigh.

'Daunting, isn't it?' murmured Mark, startling her with the accuracy of his interpretation of her thoughts.

'It's so incredibly beautiful ... yet somehow almost sinister,' she sighed.

'That's this wretched rain,' laughed Mark. 'Give them a spot of sunshine and those mountains become flamboyantly seductive.'

Lucy gave him a slightly bemused glance, wondering if he had any inkling of how often he confounded her with such unexpected remarks.

'Mark, you will let me know when you want me to drive,' she offered, relieved by and wanting to maintain the thaw in the atmosphere between them but silently praying he would refuse her offer. Being a passenger was bad enough, but the thought of getting stuck behind one of those lorries didn't appeal in the least—and the idea of trying to overtake one appealed even less.

'Perhaps later, when we're on the coastal toll road,' he muttered then, as the rain turned once more to a slushy sleet, added morosely, 'That is, if this doesn't hem us in before we make it to Valencia.' He flashed her a quick look. 'We'll stop off at the next town. We can have a coffee and something to eat. I'd also like to make a phone call.'

'About your father?' she blurted out, and felt decidedly foolish the instant she had.

'What makes you ask that?'

'It's just that you didn't actually say which day he was being operated on, though from what you said I realised it could be around today...and I woke up thinking about him this morning.'

'I couldn't remember whether I'd told you the exact day or not,' he muttered. 'I've worked it out that he should have been out of the operating theatre for some while now——'

'You mean it *was* today?' gasped Lucy.

He nodded. 'Lucy, one thing that was made clear to both him and your mother was that the risks were negligible, even though it's quite a hefty operation. They say that Dad's in remarkably good shape despite the effects of that first bout of surgery. So there really isn't anything to worry about.'

They stopped off at a small café that from the outside looked decidedly dingy. Inside it was rustic, cosy and spotless.

'Are you hungry?' he asked as they selected a table.

Lucy shook her head. 'I'll just have a coffee.'

'OK, we can stop off later for dinner. I'll see if there's a telephone I can use,' he said. 'Are you sure you wouldn't like a snack of any sort?'

Lucy shook her head, then watched as he made his way to the bar around which several men stood, chatting quietly among themselves as they drank tiny glasses of black coffee and sipped drinks. She found it rather odd that there weren't any women present, then was distracted by a small pang of envy as she heard Mark address the barman. She knew his French and Italian were fluent and, judging by the speed with which he had slipped into relaxed conversation with the men around him, his Spanish probably was too. She pulled a small face as she thought of her own very flawed French—the only foreign language she was in any way familiar with.

The soft murmurings of laughter from around the bar dragged her away from her deflating thoughts and she looked up to see Mark approaching her with a cup of coffee in his hand.

'I'll be with you in a moment,' he said, handing her the cup. 'I'll just make that call.'

'What are they finding so amusing?' asked Lucy as the men round the bar smiled over in their direction.

Mark shrugged, laughter in his eyes. 'The barman asked me if I'd bring the coffee over to you,' he murmured. 'He was afraid it might not be to your satisfaction.'

Looking puzzled, but not wishing to offend inadvertently, Lucy took a sip of the coffee and smiled her appreciation over to the watching barman. She nearly choked as her action brought discreet cheers and laughter all around.

'I've a feeling all this has something to do with the state of my eye—and their assumption that you were responsible for it,' he stated in deadpan tones.

'Perhaps you should explain that I wasn't,' she murmured, chuckling. 'Otherwise I might be tempted to give you a matching pair.'

Whatever it was that Mark said to his companions when he returned, they turned and raised their glasses to her in smiling salute. Lucy returned the compliment by raising her coffee-cup, deciding that, if this relaxed and friendly atmosphere proved typical, the chances were she might end up enjoying herself after all.

But it was when the telephone was eventually brought to Mark at the bar and he began dialling that Lucy's feelings of cosy well-being began faltering. Of course James would be all right, she told herself, her eyes raking Mark's features for any signs of her own sudden jitteriness and finding nothing. It was his father, she reassured herself as the men around him suddenly fell silent, and, if he wasn't worried, there was no earthly reason for her to be either.

She leaned forward as he began speaking into the receiver, trying with no success to hear what he was saying, her eyes frantic and pleading as he suddenly turned and faced her fully.

'They're just putting me through to the surgeon,' he called over to her, and it was then that she saw past the relaxed reassurance of his smile to the inner tension in the rigid stance of his tall body.

She leapt to her feet and raced over to him.

'Hello? Yes, that's right...his son.' As he spoke he reached out an arm to Lucy, placing it around her shoulders and drawing her closer to him. 'Is that so?'

Lucy felt her heart skip several beats in its relief at hearing the disbelieving laughter in his voice.

'That's great... No, I understand, and I wasn't expecting to be able to speak to him anyway... Yes, if you'd do that. And let him know Lucy called too.'

'And that she sends her love!' instructed Lucy indignantly.

There was laughter, relief and delight on his face when he replaced the receiver then hugged her tightly to him in silence.

'I'm so glad he's all right,' whispered Lucy, scarcely aware how close she was to tears as she hugged him back.

'Half an hour after he came round he was demanding to be let home for a decent meal,' laughed Mark as he released her.

'And demanding loudly, I'm sure!' exclaimed Lucy delightedly.

'Very,' he chuckled, picking up his coffee-cup and draining it. 'Which seems to confirm his surgeon's claim that they couldn't have wished for things to have gone any better.'

He paid for their drinks and the call, after which they made their protracted farewells.

'You know, I've a feeling I'm really going to love Spain,' sighed Lucy when they were back in the car.

'What gives you that feeling?' asked Mark as he switched on the ignition.

'Getting such good news about your father, for a start,' she replied. 'And those people being so welcoming.'

'The Spanish are an exceptionally welcoming people altogether,' he murmured. 'But are you actually saying you wouldn't have felt you'd like the country if the news about my father hadn't been so good?'

'No, of course I'm not!' exclaimed Lucy, completely thrown by the unexpected harshness of his tone. 'I meant... oh, forget it! Why do you always have to spoil everything by being so... so damned contentious?'

'Probably because I have such an unpleasant nature,' he drawled in reply.

Lucy felt herself go rigid with resentment and disbelief. Scant minutes ago he had been hugging her with delight—and now this!

'Perhaps my statement wasn't the most logical I've ever uttered,' she stated frigidly, 'but I wasn't feeling particularly logical—I was feeling happy, for heaven's sake! And don't you try denying you were over the moon to hear about your father. It was only natural for you to worry, no matter how optimistic the doctors had been. But if there's one thing I can't abide, it's men who carry on as though any expression of emotion in some way detracts from their masculinity!'

'Have you quite finished?' he demanded icily.

'Quite—thank you,' she retorted, more than a little startled by the vehemence of her attack now that it was over.

'Good, because I'll tell you something that I can't abide,' he informed her. 'It's women who dish out psychological claptrap such as you just have. Of course I was worried about my father. But wringing my hands and making a spectacle of myself wouldn't have lessened that worry one iota.'

'Just forget what I said, will you?' she exclaimed bitterly. 'The chances are I'll loathe Spain anyway—you could make paradise seem like hell!'

'It seems to me your priorities need a bit of sorting out,' he informed her in distinctly bored tones. 'I'm supposed to be the wicked stepbrother, remember? It's lovers who are meant to have the power of making your life heaven or hell or whatever else. No wonder you don't consider yourself ready for marriage yet.'

'I can hardly believe I'm hearing this,' croaked Lucy. 'Are you actually claiming that, just because you've been making my life hell ever since I was a child, you consider yourself equally capable of making it heaven? That's the most warped example of logic I've ever heard. And it only goes to show how ignorant you are about love, which, believe it or not, isn't about making other people miserable!'

'I've never claimed to know anything about love,' he retorted, 'but it's obvious I know a darned sight more about it than you do. All the great love stories read like the plot of an opera, for heaven's sake—all gloom and destruction and above all misery! And what about the alleged love of your life?' he enquired with relish. 'He loves you and you love him, yet here you are with me instead of honeymooning with him... I wouldn't think the poor guy's exactly a bundle of joy right now, would you?'

'Well, you're wrong, he's perfectly happy,' retorted Lucy defensively.

'Oh—so he wasn't that deeply in love with you after all?'

'Of course he was... is.'

'If that's the case, the man's not right in the head, letting you take off like this with someone like me.'

'Why should he see someone like you as a threat?' she blurted out, then decided to qualify that reckless question before he had a chance to answer it. 'Especially when I've agreed to live with him once I return.'

'But you've still not agreed to marry him?'

'Not for a while,' she muttered, wondering just how much more embroidery she would be obliged to add to this ridiculous tale.

'And he really didn't object to your coming to Spain with me?'

'Why should he—it's my job, isn't it?'

'Something tells me you haven't exactly been honest as to the nature of our relationship,' he murmured, with a touch of smugness that made Lucy's blood boil.

'He's perfectly aware of our relationship,' she retorted hotly. 'Now, would you mind dropping this subject? It's none of your business anyway!'

'I'd guess he knows that I'm your boss and your stepbrother,' he continued relentlessly. 'But what about that rather disturbing sexual chemistry that's so disconcertingly manifested itself between us of late?'

Lucy clamped her lips tightly shut: that sexual chemistry was yet another to add to the list of subjects away from which she was so desperately trying to steer her thoughts.

'Lucy?'

'Shut up!' she hissed, hating him for the hornets' nest he had stirred up in her mind.

She *did* find him devastatingly sexually attractive; and, though he had the power to make her life hell at times, he was undoubtedly also linked to the crazy sense of exhilaration she had experienced last night on the boat. It was her ridiculous optimism that had made her ignore all evidence to the contrary and view the prospect of falling in love as something joyous and pain-free, she told herself accusingly. Yet if love was the unmitigated misery Mark claimed it to be and which, she admitted with a small shudder, the ghastly experiences some of her friends had suffered seemed to prove it to be, then the odds were that she was head over heels in love with him—and probably had been for a depressing number of years!

'Am I to take it that this determination of yours not even to discuss the subject indicates that you haven't actually come clean with—what was his name—George?'

'And exactly how honest have you been with—what's her name—Andrea?' she flung back rashly.

'Lucy, there's no possible comparison,' he retorted. 'My relationship with Andrea is entirely different.'

'Oh, I'm sure it is,' she exclaimed witheringly. 'The difference being that you, the male, are entitled to be as secretive as you like over such matters—whereas I, the lowly female, am required to divulge all!'

'Naturally, there is that aspect to it,' he murmured drily, 'but what I actually meant was that I'm not planning on setting up house with Andrea, or any other woman, for that matter, and especially not with a view to an eventual marriage.'

'But I'm sure, had you been, you would have told her,' retorted Lucy with scathing scepticism.

'One thing I can absolutely guarantee is that if ever I meet a woman with whom I'd contemplate marriage the question of my being sexually attracted to someone else simply wouldn't arise.'

Lucy turned involuntarily and glanced at his profile, shadowed and inscrutable in the faintly glowing light emanating from the dashboard. He glanced momentarily in her direction.

'You look as though you don't believe me,' he stated, his words followed by a curiously hollow laugh.

The trouble was that she did believe him, she thought dejectedly as the possibility of being in love with him began nagging away at her like a relentlessly aching tooth.

'The trouble is, I've no right to expect you to have any more understanding of what makes me tick than you have of me,' he stated suddenly. 'The fact that we've been technically related for a number of years because our parents happened to marry doesn't alter the fact that we probably both have acquaintances we understand better than we do one another.'

'It's only very recently that I've been able to understand why you resented me so much,' Lucy found herself admitting.

'You feel I resented you?' he enquired with an edge of sarcasm. 'God, you were lucky that's all you felt! To saddle a twenty-two-year-old with any measure of responsibility for the sort of brat you were was asking for all manner of trouble!'

'I must say there were times when I wondered if you weren't about to throttle me...and I can't honestly say I'd blame you if you had—not then, anyway. But I stopped being that brat quite a number of years ago.'

'Yet I still show signs of wanting to throttle you?'

'It's not just you—it's me too,' she exclaimed earnestly, determined not to let this unique opportunity slip from her grasp. 'The moment you start laying down the law to me, I feel myself reverting back to that fifteen-year-old brat—my mind freezes on me and I find it impossible to think either coherently or logically...and I end up feeling like a gibbering juvenile.'

'And I end up wanting to throttle you,' he murmured with a throaty chuckle. 'Lucy, do you honestly think I'm not aware of this effect we have on one another?'

She gave a defeated shrug, but said nothing. Perhaps unravelling the antagonism of the past wasn't such a good idea, she thought dejectedly, because without them what was she left with? As a teenager she had had her one and only crush on him...and as an adult her only true inkling of the frightening potential of her as yet untapped sexuality had been discovered in his arms.

'But we both know what happens when I try blotting out the past and treat you as the woman you undoubtedly are,' he suddenly added grimly.

'Are you saying that you're incapable of responding to a woman in any other way than sexually?' she demanded, bitterly resenting that her attempt at honesty had only resulted in furthering her confusion.

'How would you react if I were to ask you if you responded to every man who took you in his arms as you did to me?' he demanded harshly. 'And don't give me any of that drivel about its cause being the terrific sex life you'd had with someone else!'

Lucy flashed him a look of pure loathing as she inwardly squirmed at the reminder of such a ludicrous claim.

'Tell me—will this George be the first man you've actually lived with?' he demanded.

'No.' As she calmly uttered the lie she found herself wondering what his reaction would be to the truth—that not only had she never lived with a man, but also she had never really been seriously tempted to enter into a physical relationship with any of the ones with whom she had been romantically involved.

'So—exactly how many men have you lived with?' he enquired, the faint note of censure in his tone incensing her.

'Mind your own damned business!'

'Perhaps you're right, that wasn't my business, but——'

'There's absolutely no "perhaps" about it!'

'But what if I choose to make the question of your moving in with George my business?' he persisted as though she had never interrupted.

Lucy struggled to contain her fury as she rounded on him. 'The question of your having any choice regarding the matter simply doesn't arise.'

'Which of us are you trying to kid, Lucy?' he taunted softly. 'Not me, I hope.'

'What's there to kid anyone about?' she demanded in a voice that betrayed miraculously little of her mounting feelings of panic. 'When I return to England I'm going to live with George—and that's all there is to it!'

'You're that certain, are you, that anything that might develop between us in the meantime would be conveniently over and done with by then?' he asked, his words devoid of any expression.

'I didn't... Mark, I...' Her words choked to a halt as everything within her seemed to race out of control.

'What—no denials that something might actually happen between us?' he drawled.

'I'm certainly not denying that... that some perverse sort of attraction seems to have arisen between us,' she stammered, part of her mind resorting to attempting to convince her this nightmarish conversation wasn't really taking place. 'But it's something that neither of us welcomes in the least.'

'True,' he conceded with a grim laugh. 'But on the other hand I doubt if either of us much welcomes the idea of remaining locked in that ludicrous time-warp where I'm the antagonistically resentful guardian and you're the scheming brat. Yet we both know what the consequences are likely to be of our trying to escape from it.'

'No, we don't!' she protested, far too vehemently for her own liking. 'For heaven's sake, Mark, you make it sound as though...' She broke off, uncertain how to phrase her thoughts, then continued from a safer angle. 'You seem to have overlooked the fact that we've managed to work together as reasonable adults...and besides, I'm in love with George.' She felt herself cringe as she heard those last words, wondering what on earth had possessed her to utter them.

'Dear me, Lucy, do I detect a slight cooling in your affections towards poor old George?' he enquired with syrupy concern. 'Not so long ago you were claiming to be *deeply* in love with him.'

Lucy flashed him her most murderous look, even though she knew it to be wasted in the virtual darkness enveloping them.

'But I suppose there will be one consolation, should our good intentions come to nothing,' he continued unconcernedly. 'At least it will be nothing more than good old-fashioned lust we'll be dealing with. I hear love complicates such matters no end—though I dare say you know all about that.'

Lucy leaned back against her seat, her eyes closing. She had no experience of the complications created by love...but the chill sensation of foreboding crawling its way throughout her seemed to be telling her that soon she could well be experiencing it to the hilt.

CHAPTER EIGHT

IT WAS approaching eleven o'clock when they eventually stopped for a meal, by which time the very idea of food made Lucy feel slightly nauseous.

After they had driven for several hours in tense silence, their exchanges concerning the meal were explosively acrimonious.

'Damn it, if you can't understand the menu all you have to do is say so and I'll translate it for you!' grumbled Mark at the onset.

'There's no need for you to—I shan't be eating!'

'For heaven's sake, stop being so childish!'

'I'm not being childish—I'm not hungry!'

'And to think I was worried it was lack of food making you incapable of speech for the past few hours!'

'Obviously it wouldn't occur to you that it might simply be a lack of interest in conversing with you,' hissed Lucy, the last words they exchanged until he had eaten his way through a meal comprising several elaborate courses.

'I suppose it's a waste of breath to ask if you'd like coffee,' he muttered when he had at last finished.

'No, it isn't—I'd like some.'

'My, you are making a pig of yourself,' he observed sarcastically when she then had a second cup.

'I'm going to need it for my stint of driving,' she informed him sweetly, feeling quite secure in the knowledge there was little chance of his even considering letting her drive in such appalling conditions. 'I shall be driving when we leave here, shan't I?'

He gave her a shrivelling look before uttering the words she had secretly been relying on.

'If you think I'd let you get your first taste of driving a right-hand-drive car here in these conditions, you're mad.'

It was with a decided twinge of guilt at the thought of the number of unrelieved hours he had actually been driving in these dreadful conditions that Lucy once again got into the passenger-seat of the car. But they resumed their journey in the same charged silence in which they had broken it—a silence that hung between them un-disturbed during the relentless hours it took for them finally to reach their water-logged destination.

'Now all we need is to find that the caretaker hasn't got the place ready for us—or has forgotten to leave a key,' muttered Mark as, in deluging rain, they sped the few steps from the car to the arched veranda running along the front of the austerely whitewashed though ex-tremely elegant building standing in a clearing sur-rounded by acres of citrus groves.

'Stop being such a pessimist,' chided Lucy, her words softened by the sight of the stark exhaustion on his gaunt face, down which rivulets of rain sped unchecked. 'I'm sure all these outside lights wouldn't have been left on unless we were expected.'

He gave a desultory look around him, while Lucy hugged her arms around her, her teeth chattering with the cold.

'Well, there's no mat to leave a key under,' muttered Mark, trying the wrought-iron handle of the ornate security grille barring the entrance door. 'One down, one to go,' he said as the grille opened, then rolled his eyes in disbelief as he tried the huge entrance door and it too opened. 'Impressive security.'

'What about the luggage?' asked Lucy, hesitating before entering—all she wanted was to get into her nightclothes and a bed and sleep forever.

'I'll get it in a minute,' said Mark, ushering her impatiently into the darkened house. 'Where the hell is the light switch?' Lucy heard him mutter beside her as her nostrils were suddenly filled by the lightest, most pleasing of scents.

Her unaccustomed eyes blinked furiously as light suddenly filled the long hallway stretching out before her, then widened in delight as they alighted on a beautifully carved dark wood table on which stood a magnificent vase from which spilled a riotous profusion of flowers— the source of that freshly welcoming scent first assailing her.

'How lovely,' she sighed with involuntary delight. 'I'd no idea it would be anything like this!'

'I suppose, as halls go, it's an absolute knockout,' observed Mark sourly. 'But would you mind leaving your domesticated ooings and ahings till the morning and see if you can find a couple of rooms with beds made up? Meanwhile, I'll get a few things from the car.'

Too exhausted even to feel a twinge of resentment at such deflating lack of enthusiasm, Lucy made her way down the hall in search of somewhere to sleep.

She was almost dead on her feet, she thought wearily—so what on earth must Mark be feeling like? As she sketchily explored the place to get her bearings, she saw that the house comprised a huge rectangle surrounding an inner courtyard and found herself looking forward to a more thorough exploration once she had a good night's sleep behind her. Across the front of the house ran the living areas, and running parallel across the back was the kitchen and utility section. The two sides of the house contained the sleeping quarters and bathrooms, each section consisting of two huge bedrooms, between which, and servicing both, was a palatial bathroom. Only the bedrooms on one side of the house had been prepared, their large beds immaculately made up with dazzling white bed-linen and covers.

'Did you have any success?' he called to her.

Lucy made her way down the marbled corridor bounding the inner courtyard and back to the hall.

'There are two bedrooms made up in that wing,' she told him, nodding back towards where she had just come from as she walked up to him. 'Heavens, Mark, you look exhausted,' she exclaimed involuntarily, an aching softness melting through her at the sight of his rain-drenched, battered face. 'And your eye, if anything, looks worse than it did this morning. Shall I see if I can find something to put on it?'

He shook his head, his eyebrows rising in mocking query.

'Miracle man though you obviously take me to be, even I find it difficult to look my fresh and beautiful best when I've a dozen or so hours of concentrated driving in gale conditions behind me,' he drawled, then turned his attention to the luggage at his feet. 'Here, take this,' he said, handing her a holdall. 'And lead me to one of those bedrooms, where I intend getting twenty-four hours' uninterrupted sleep.'

'I know exactly what you mean,' sympathised Lucy, leading the way. 'That's how I feel and I didn't even have any driving to contend with.'

'True,' he muttered, shouldering open the door to the first bedroom. 'Perhaps I'd better be left to sleep for forty-eight hours, just to be on the safe side.' He turned as he heaved his luggage through the door. 'Have you what you'll require for the night in that holdall—or would you like me to get the rest of your things?'

'This is fine, thank you,' she replied, suddenly feeling awkward and tongue-tied on top of the anxiety still niggling away at her over his physical state. 'Well... goodnight, then.'

She made her way down the corridor to the second of the bedrooms, conscious of a constricting tightness within her as she entered, dropped her holdall on the floor and began stripping off her sodden clothing.

She didn't feel... well, right, she thought disconsolately as she drew back the pristine white bedspread and flung herself down on the bed. She couldn't even find a more dramatic word than 'right', she complained miserably to herself, but, whatever it was, she never felt right or herself or anything even remotely normal whenever Mark was around.

She pillowed her face on her arms and listened to the howl of the wind and the lash of the rain. Despite both, it wasn't in the least cold in the room—yet she was shivering from head to toe. She felt this way because she was damp and worn out, she rationalised wearily...either that, or she was terrified out of her wits by the idea of loving Mark.

She rolled on to her back and gazed sightlessly up at the high, whitewashed ceiling, her head shaking slowly from side to side as though in private argument. There was a limit as to how long she could go on kidding herself she wasn't in love with him, she finally conceded, and immediately experienced the sensation of an unbearable weight falling away from her. The whys and the wherefores of it all were completely irrelevant at this stage, she told herself fatalistically; throughout her life she had unwittingly found herself embroiled in disasters—though this one was definitely the most disastrous of them all.

Facing reality wasn't going to produce any longed-for miracles, she reasoned carefully, but at least it should go some way to unscrambling a mind too long confused by its ostrich-like refusal to face the facts.

But there were other less comforting aspects of facing reality, such as the fiercely protective ache of anxiety filling her as an image of his weary, damaged face leapt to her mind; and then the hot, sharp sweetness of a terrible need stabbing through her as she relived those moments in his arms...

She woke with a start, the chill stiffness of her body as she struggled upright telling her she had slept for some while.

Groggy with sleep, she rose and stripped down to her bra and pants, then rummaged through the holdall for her washbag and stumbled towards the bathroom.

A quick going over of her teeth and then she would sleep forever, she promised herself as she entered the

cool, palatial bathroom. Moorish, she thought as she
sleepily searched through her washbag for her tooth-
brush. The whole place, she now realised, was designed
along those sparsely elegant, yet almost contradictorily
exotic, Moorish lines.

Intrigued, she glanced round her lavish surroundings—then gave a shriek of fright, her washbag
clattering to the gleaming floor as she caught sight of
Mark. He was seated on the wide rim of a huge semi-
sunken bath, one towel draped around his hips, another
draped over his head. What filled her with terror was
the way his broad, darkly tanned shoulders were slumped
against the tiled wall behind him.

'Mark, what happened?' she cried, racing to him.

His powerful body shifted sluggishly as his hands rose,
lifting the towel covering his head a fraction.

'Lucy?' he muttered groggily.

He was about to die on her, she thought in heart-
stopping panic. She loved him and now he was about
to die on her!

'Mark, I . . .' She clamped shut her mouth as she tried
to regain a semblance of control over herself. Blurting
out that she loved him would probably give him a cor-
onary! 'Mark, don't try to move,' she pleaded in a trembling voice, her hands reaching out to the towel from
beneath which he was peering at her in dazed bewilderment. 'Is there a phone here? How do I get hold of
a doctor?'

'Why? What's wrong?' he muttered, alarm creeping
into his slurred words.

'Mark, can you remember what happened to you?'
she asked, striving to keep the terror from her voice.

'Of course I can.'

'Thank God for that! Is it your head?'

'Is what my head?' he asked.

'Mark, you have to tell me what happened!'

'I had a shower and washed my hair—I must have dozed off,' he exclaimed impatiently. 'Lucy——'

'Dozed off?' she croaked. 'You mean you didn't have a blackout or something?'

For an instant he looked at her in blank amazement, then a sleepy smile crept to his lips.

'No—I didn't have a blackout...or anything.'

'Oh,' she gulped, feeling suddenly limp and deflated. 'For a moment I thought you had.'

'Well, I hadn't.'

And it had been on the tip of her tongue to tell him how much she loved him, she thought dazedly, then suddenly became aware of her arms, raised to his head, their wrists still trapped in his hands. It was then that her eyes began their startling journey down her body, at first encountering the lacy blackness of her bra clinging to the smooth swell of her breasts, and then the black lace triangle of her bikini pants.

Refusing to take in what they were seeing, her eyes moved over to the towel slung around the lean masculine hips so close to hers... Small though that towel was, a sanctimonious voice inside her informed her, it covered a darned sight more of him than those flimsy bits of lace did her.

'So—you were worried about me, were you?' he enquired mockingly.

'Not particularly,' she lied, feeling like shoving him into the bath and turning on the taps for his insensitive ingratitude.

'Well, let's put it this way,' he murmured, 'if I were George—which thank God I'm not—I'd be murderously jealous to find you displaying, among other things, such concern for another man.'

As he spoke he lowered her hands to his shoulders, then tossed aside the towel that had covered his head.

'Stop it,' she pleaded weakly as he began drawing her trembling body into his arms.

'If only I could,' he whispered.

His lips were beguilingly gentle, teasing and caressing hers to an impatient hunger while his hands explored the smooth contours of her back, his fingers deftly undoing her bra the instant they encountered its obstruction. A soft chuckle of pleasure escaped him as she momentarily released him from the fierce hold of her arms to facilitate his removal of her bra.

'You're making me feel positively overdressed,' he teased huskily against her parted lips, his breath quickening as his mouth slid hotly to her throat. 'You're so beautiful,' he murmured, with such ardent delight that she felt her heart soar giddily. 'So very beautiful,' he groaned, suddenly arching her body and burying his face against the velvet smoothness of her breasts.

She dropped her cheek to his head, rubbing it distractedly against the damp darkness of his hair while her arms held him to her in unquestioning love. She had been shaken by what had been awoken in her that first time he had held her in his arms, but what she had felt then was as nothing compared to the savage urgency of the need now possessing her as his mouth teased and tormented against her aching flesh.

'Tell me that you want me, Lucy,' he whispered hoarsely, raising his head and returning his questioning mouth to hers. He drew her sharply against him, sending intense jolts of excitement jarring through her already sensation-racked body and bringing soft gasps of protesting pleasure to her lips. 'Tell me, Lucy,' he demanded, his eyes burning slits as he suddenly raised his head and gazed down at her. 'Tell me that you want me—not George, not any other man—only me!'

'Mark—don't,' she pleaded, her arms straining to draw his head back down to hers in silent love.

'Why?' he demanded harshly. 'Is this the way you feel in his arms?' he groaned, twisting his head aside as her mouth tried to reach his. 'Why won't you answer me, Lucy? Why?'

She shook her head, desperate to counteract the resistance in him, yet unable to answer for fear of the words of love threatening to pour from her.

'Why won't you explain to me how it is you can claim to love one man, yet respond like this to another?'

'Stop it!' she cried, going against every instinct in her body as she tore herself free. 'Why do you have to keep asking questions? Why can't you…?' The words choked to a halt in her as he leaned back from her in a gesture of total rejection.

'Why can't I leave well alone and simply get on with what we both want—making love to you?' he demanded harshly. 'The answer to that, my tempting Lucy, is that I'm the unfortunate possessor of a mind that refuses to let go, no matter what the dictates of my body.' He rose to his feet. 'Though, to be scrupulously honest, tonight might well have proved an exception had it not been for the fact that my body isn't exactly up to par at the moment...come to think of it, I doubt if I'd have found the physical energy required for lovemaking.'

Lucy's eyes had become transfixed on the gleaming tiles of the floor, her stunned mind not even attempting to convince her that this wasn't happening to her. It was; and never in her life again could there be a moment more destructively humiliating than this—of that she was certain. He spoke of lovemaking, but what he was referring to had nothing even remotely to do with love. Reality didn't lie in facing up to loving him, she thought numbly, it lay in facing up to what was entailed in loving a man who so openly deplored the fact that he found her desirable and a man, moreover, who regarded love as something to be ridiculed.

'Damn you, Lucy, can't you say anything?' he roared.

For an instant she froze, her mind struggling to bring her solace with a belated attempt at rejecting reality. Then she shook her head; such childish ploys were behind her—reality was here to stay. She rose unsteadily to her feet.

'Mark, I . . . oh, what's the use?' she choked, and fled to her bedroom.

'Lucy?'

Almost at the bed, she spun round, oblivious of her near-nakedness as she faced him.

'Get out of here. And don't ever come within so much as an inch of me again!'

'My God—you're crying!' he exclaimed, hitching the towel more securely around him as he strode towards her. 'Lucy, in all the years I've known you, I've never once known you to cry.'

'Yet another success you can chalk up at my expense,' she howled at him, control deserting her completely.

'Lucy, it's not like that at all,' he groaned, reaching out and hauling her into his arms. 'Our relationship has always been fraught with complications. Can't you see that I always had problems dealing with you when you were a brat? I'm still having problems, albeit completely different ones, now that you're a desirable woman!'

'You don't make me feel in the least desirable,' she accused tearfully, while her body responded to the return of his with wanton abandon.

'Don't I?' he groaned, his hands sliding sensuously down her body, moulding it to his and leaving her with no trace of doubt as to the strength of his desire for her.

She buried her face against him, her hands trembling as they explored against the muscled smoothness of his body, retreating in momentary alarm as their restless roving dislodged the towel at his hips.

'Aren't you going to complete the job?' he teased huskily, his mouth hot and hungry on hers as she recklessly tugged free the towel.

In one instant his body was shifting slightly to accommodate the fall of the towel to the floor, in the next his arms were tightening fiercely around her, his body electrifying hers to shuddering abandonment with the potent message of its needs.

'Did you not believe me when I said I might not have the stamina for this?' he demanded hoarsely, lifting her in his arms and carrying her to the bed.

'It wouldn't have mattered,' she vowed wildly, the fierce cling of her arms carrying him down with her as he placed her on the bed. 'I don't care!'

'You don't care?' he queried huskily, his hands sweeping down her body and laughter rumbling softly in his throat as her impassioned clinging rendered his removal of the last of her clothing into a major feat of dexterity on his part. 'You don't care if I gasp my last while making love to you?' he whispered, drawing her racked body to the turgid heat of his.

'Don't say that!' she choked, the memory of her earlier terror too fresh in her mind for such a joke.

'Why not? At least I'd die a blissfully happy man,' he groaned, his body tensing as though in an attempt to control the trembling urgency of the madness possessing her.

'Please,' she begged, her arms dragging his head down to hers and the mindless madness within her spilling out to him as their mouths clung in bruising passion.

There was nothing she could begin to do to contain the savage impatience now driving her, even though deep down she could sense he was attempting to resist it.

'Are you certain this is how you want it to be?' he protested raggedly.

'Yes!' There was absolute certainty in her cry which completely dismissed the inability of her mind to determine the exact meaning of his demand.

But it was that one word of submission that dissolved what was left of his resistance and unleashed the full force of the passion raging within him.

Now it was she who was racing to keep up with him, her untutored body too overwhelmed by the exquisite pleasures being inflicted on it for there to be any room in her mind for either shock at what was happening now or fear of what was to come. But both eventually put in their belated appearance, galvanised into existence in one brief, searing moment of pain that tore in a ragged cry from her lips and was answered by an enraged groan of disbelief.

'Damn you, Lucy!' he exploded. 'Damn you, damn——'

'Love me, Mark,' she pleaded, that moment of agony blotted from existence by the sudden, sharp bursts of pleasure which had begun exploding at random throughout her body.

'Love you?' he demanded, his groaned protest deteriorating into disbelieving laughter. 'How could I not?' he whispered as his body began orchestrating those random bursts of pleasure within her, slowing then quickening their pace until they overlapped and ran amok into one endless, rapturous explosion.

She heard her own incoherent cries, which were her vain attempt to tell him of what had happened to her, and heard those cries deteriorate into soft moans of delight as she felt that wondrous cycle begin erupting all over again within her.

And gradually she learned that words were unnecessary, that her body had already spoken to his with fervent eloquence and in turn had begun absorbing the secret messages of his, and did so with such faultless understanding that it was as one that passion finally encompassed them and hurtled them into the oblivion of absolute fulfilment.

Her brain staggered back to partial consciousness with the message that it wanted time to stand still; that it wanted this moment to become forever. And for eternity, this would be all that she would ask—to lie here in his arms, the warm masculine scent of him bathing her, his ragged, panted sighs, still so redolent with passion, whispering in her ears.

But as she gradually felt her own tortured lungs return to something approaching normal, she was forced reluctantly to accept that time had moved uncooperatively on and that any second now she was going to have to face a music far more discordant than any she had ever encountered before.

When he moved he did so swiftly and with deliberate purpose; one moment their bodies were entwined, the next, not only were they apart, but he had placed as much distance as the bed would allow between them. He lay stretched out on his stomach, his head cushioned on his arms and his eyes baleful as they watched her.

'Why don't you take one of the pillows and place that between us too?' she demanded in defiant response to the crippling feelings of desolation pervading her.

'I'd say it was a bit late for that—wouldn't you?' he drawled, his eyes icy as they maintained their unblinking watch on her. 'Why did you lie to me?'

'I'm not sure I know what you mean.' Her heart lurched sickeningly as she realised that her reflexive response was probably about the worst she could possibly have made.

'Even among the string of lies you've been telling me, I'm damn sure you know which particular one I'm referring to right now!' he roared, then buried his face in his arms with a groaned sigh. 'Lucy, I don't want this to deteriorate into a shouting match.'

'Well, stop shouting at me, then!'

'But for once in my life I'm completely at a loss for words—I just don't know what to make of any of this.'

Scant moments ago she had wanted time to stand still in this man's arms, she thought, dazed and hurt; she loved him and had given the fullest expression possible to him of that love . . . and now he was telling her he didn't know what to make of it. If he was that blind and insensitive, he didn't deserve her or anyone else's love!

'For heaven's sake, Mark, I can't see your problem,' she exclaimed, her words light, her heart leaden. 'All we did was make love.'

'Oh, yes—all we did was make love,' he jeered, rising to his elbows and scowling at her. 'And we both know what a hectic sex life you're used to. What sort of blind fool do you take me for if you think I didn't realise tonight was the first time?'

'I don't think that!' she flung at him bitterly. 'But I did think that was the sort of thing most men were inclined to crow over—not complain about!'

She gave a shriek of terror as he lunged across the bed at her and grabbed her painfully by the shoulders.

'Which doesn't say much for the type of men you mix with—though God only knows what sort they are!' he roared. 'And you might as well accept the fact that I'm going to get to the truth behind all this, even if I have to wring it out of you!'

'Mark, why are you behaving like this?' she croaked, the fear that he actually would carry out his threat stark in her voice.

'Because you lied to me! Because you told me in no uncertain terms that you were sexually experienced!'

'All right—so I wasn't,' she choked. 'You're the one always accusing me of lying to you, so what's so special this time? I'd have thought you'd be used to it by now.'

He released her with a groan of exasperation, then flopped down beside her.

'Lucy, even I am having difficulty believing you can be quite this stupid,' he protested. 'This time I need to know *why* you lied. I want to know exactly what it was in that devious, scheming little mind of yours that led you to this and landed me in such a wretched mess!'

Had he hit her, beaten her to a pulp, he would never have inflicted as much damage on her as those callous words had. If he considered himself to be in a wretched mess now, she thought grimly, what sort of mess would he describe himself as being in if he learned the truth? For one vengeful moment she was tempted to hurl the truth at him—just for the satisfaction of seeing the horror on his face. A bitter, choked laugh escaped her as she accepted not only that her pride would never allow her such satisfaction, but that it was stupidity on her part even to imagine he would ever believe her.

'You have a problem, Mark,' she informed him tonelessly. 'How could you ever be certain I actually was telling you the truth—even if I were?'

'Try me,' he snapped.

She had to come up with something, she thought, but what? It was as though everything had died within her and all that was left was one last stubborn spark of pride.

'I was sick and tired of your treating me as though I were a child,' she began, then her mind froze on her, refusing to go on.

'Hang on a moment,' he muttered, unintentionally offering her respite. 'Does this George character actually exist?'

She shook her head, even that requiring considerable effort on her part.

'Why did you invent him?'

'I've no idea . . . I just did on the spur of the moment.'

'Because you knew that there was no way I'd get sexually involved with you if I knew you were a virgin,' he muttered grimly.

Sexually involved? Her mind reeled at the inimical coldness of the term, and not only that—anyone would think, from the way he was carrying on, that she had roped him down and ravished him uninvited!

'Nothing of the sort occurred to me!' she rounded on him in an explosive outburst of hurt and fury. 'I'd no idea you'd have such kinked views on the subject!'

'Give me strength,' he groaned softly, rolling his eyes heavenwards. 'I take it you've never attempted lovemaking before?'

'Of course I haven't,' she exclaimed indignantly before her shock at such a question gave way to confusion. 'What do you mean—attempted?'

'A complete lack of physical experience in a woman isn't necessarily that obvious to a man,' he informed her quietly.

She closed her eyes and wished she could close her ears too. The most beautiful thing that had ever happened to her was now being coldly and clinically dissected by the man with whom she had just shared that experience.

'Lucy, do you think I'm not aware of how appallingly I'm handling this?' he asked softly.

Her eyes flew open in shock at the startling change in his tone, the breath catching painfully in her throat as she glimpsed unmistakable tenderness doing battle with the harshness of his expression.

'Your lack of experience was exceptionally obvious,' he whispered contritely. 'Can't you understand that, had I known, I might have avoided hurting you quite so much?'

'It only lasted a second,' she whispered, a crazy feeling akin to hope awakening in her.

'But that isn't the point,' he protested. 'Oh, hell—come here,' he muttered, rolling onto his back and drawing her to his side. 'Lucy, the point I'm trying to make is that just because things worked out the way they did and we ended up making the most incredible love imaginable——'

'What did you just say?' she croaked, life flooding riotously back into her.

'Don't tell me you had any doubts on that score,' he murmured, laughter softening the words.

'Not on my part,' she blurted out recklessly. 'But I wanted to tell you . . . I tried to tell you . . .'

'And you succeeded,' he chuckled softly. 'You most certainly succeeded . . . But this isn't getting us anywhere,' he exclaimed, his tone hardening. 'Lucy, it's almost dawn and we're both dead beat—and for those reasons alone I'm dropping this right now.' He removed his arm from around her and sat up. 'But don't think

I'm not aware that you've given me nothing even approaching the truth.' He rose from the bed, bronzed and beautiful and completely at ease with his nakedness. 'Whatever it is you're up to—I'll get it out of you.' There was a lazy smile on his lips as he squatted beside the bed and took one of her hands in his. Her heart lurched in dizzy delight when he raised that hand to his lips. 'I've a feeling that getting the truth out of you by making love to you will be so much easier than by shouting at you,' he murmured. 'And so much more exciting,' he added, leaning over and kissing her softly on the mouth.

She had just about overcome the pride forbidding her to beg him to stay, but by then he was already making his way to his own room through the linking bathroom.

CHAPTER NINE

FOR the first three days he neither shouted at her nor made love to her. It was as though he had shelved his plans to extract the truth from her while he got them both into the routine best suited to what he plainly regarded as the most important facet of his life—his work.

Yet, in the days since their working routine had become fully established, he still hadn't even once attempted to cross-examine her, thought Lucy, turning in her chair to gaze morosely round the exotically elegant room set aside for office purposes.

With an audible sigh she returned her attention to entering up the mass of technical data Mark had recorded before leaving for one of his interminable meetings. She had almost acquired the knack of splitting her mind in two, one half dealing with her work, the other drifting restlessly from one aspect to the next of the subject now dominating virtually her every waking moment—Mark. She had almost acquired the knack, but not quite, her body reminded her with a sudden aching awareness; the odd line of gibberish that had appeared in the work she had printed out for him on the fourth day had shattered the eerie peace between them ... and had led ultimately to their spending the rest of the day locked in the devastating magic of making love.

She entered the last of the dictation, removed the earphones and began printing out the work, stark desolation darkening her features. And that was what was so unbearable...so mind-blowingly surreal about everything, she thought defeatedly; those isolated excursions into the realms of magic from an existence so disturbingly and uncompromisingly oppressive that at times she feared for her sanity.

Her slim body seemed to shrink as she leaned back against her chair. There was nothing she could do, no one she could turn to simply to help restore her diminishing grasp on reality. The remote graciousness of her beautiful yet alien surroundings only served to make her feel isolated and vulnerable, as did the fact that her complete lack of Spanish made it impossible even to exchange a few words with the friendly young woman who arrived to do the housework each morning, bearing the fresh milk and bread and other produce on which Mark and she would snack during the day before invariably eating out for their evening meal.

She remembered with a sharp pang of longing the welcoming atmosphere in the unpretentious little bar at which they had stopped off during their journey down. That was the Spain she longed to know, not those exclusive, prohibitively expensive and utterly soulless places in which they'd been dining each night. In fact, she reflected bitterly, the closest she had come to experiencing a warmth and friendliness similar to that first night had been at the bank, of all places, to which Mark had taken her after having decided it might be expedient for her to be able to sign company cheques in case such a need arose.

She gazed heavy-eyed at the printer whirring quietly beside her...part of her problem was that she was incapable of accepting that any of this was really happening to her. But it was! And Mark was the coldhearted, calculating instigator of it all—deliberately isolating her from any of the warmth she felt to be an integral part of Spain while one moment burning her with the fierceness of his passion and the next freezing her with the ice in his heart. Their lovemaking was always random and explosive, sometimes triggered by no more than a chance meeting of their eyes, yet never once had he spent an entire night with her—a calculated attempt on his part, she was certain, to humiliate her... Except that it never had, she reminded herself with a pang of relief, because in her heart of hearts she knew there was a need in him for her as great as, if not greater than, hers for him. It was a need she found inexplicable, but which also troubled her deeply in that, unlike hers, it had no bearing whatsoever on love.

She straightened suddenly in the chair, her body tensing painfully as her mind inexplicably resurrected a picture of herself entering his room all those years ago and finding him in bed with a woman... and how many others had there been since? she asked herself tormentedly, raising her trembling hands to her face and rubbing them distractedly against her cheeks as the flawless face of Andrea Stuart filled her mind.

Deep down she had actually allowed herself to believe that, no matter how bizarre the circumstances, what they had together was unique. As unique as all the rest of them, she told herself with bitter self-disgust. Whereas she was driven by love, *his* response stemmed from nothing more than a powerful sexual drive, and no doubt he had been every bit as passionately intense in his lovemaking with every one of those women for as long as they had attracted him . . . which had never been for particularly long.

'It's late—I'd no idea you'd still be slaving away in here.'

Lucy almost leapt out of her skin with the shock of hearing his voice.

'I didn't hear you,' she muttered.

'What's this—the report?' he asked, glancing at the printer as he approached the beautifully carved table she was using as a desk, then leaning against it and gazing down at her.

'Yes. I'm just printing it off.'

She hadn't even consciously looked at him, yet her eyes had managed to take a complete inventory of him, she thought resentfully, and, not only that, her heart was pounding and her stomach careering drunkenly all over the place—just because this black-hearted monster had shown up!

'What do you think of it?' he asked.

'It seems fine,' she retorted coldly; she hated times like these when he managed almost to sound normal— too often they had stirred hope in her.

'I thought you'd be interested in the idea of strictly organic methods being used here—perhaps it's the proposed clinic being run on alternative lines you're not too taken with?'

'I told you—it all seems fine,' snapped Lucy. What he was describing would most certainly have interested and impressed her had she been in anything approaching her normal state of mind, but it appalled her to think that her mind had become so completely detached that nothing of what she had been working on for long hours had managed to penetrate it.

'Is there something wrong?' he asked, his tone more wary than concerned.

Lucy gazed up at him with a dazzlingly false smile. 'What could possibly be wrong?'

'Things are getting to you, are they, darling?' he drawled, reaching out and placing a hand on her shoulder. 'Perhaps you'd feel better if you got a few things off your chest.' As he spoke his hand slid slowly down to her breast.

Lucy kicked back her chair, staggering to her feet as she slapped aside his hand.

'How about if we skip dinner and go straight to bed?' he suggested, his tone unruffled.

'I've no intention of skipping dinner,' she replied icily, though thrown by his words; sex was normally an explosively spontaneous occurrence between them, never mentioned and certainly never planned.

'OK—we'll have an early dinner near by—then we'll go to bed.'

'But that wouldn't be fair on you,' she murmured with sugary sweetness, her mind jangling with suspicion—he was up to something, but she had no idea what. 'You work such long hours during the day and it's really not fair that you should be put to all that inconvenience of having to wake yourself up in the small hours of the night and sneak off to your own room—so forget it!'

'Ah, so that's what's bothering you—the fact that I don't choose to spend the entire night in your seductive arms.'

Lucy gripped the back of the chair tightly, certain that if it hadn't been such a weight she would have picked it up and smashed it over his head.

'It doesn't bother me in the least,' she managed stiffly. 'But even you would have to admit it's a pretty peculiar way to conduct a relationship.'

'A relationship?' he enquired mildly, the dark curve of his eyebrows rising in mocking amusement.

'What, exactly, would you call it—if not a relationship?' she exploded as the full force of his insult hit savagely home.

'I was under the impression that the term "relationship", in that context, implied at least a modicum of trust,' he stated mildly. 'Whereas you're fully aware that not only do I not trust you, I also haven't the slightest idea why you picked on me to be your first lover. Don't for one moment think that I'm not appreciative of such an honour.' He broke off, his eyes flickering lasciviously down her body. 'But it's an honour which, I should point out, I find dubious and can only regard with the deepest of suspicion.'

Lucy's grip on the chair tightened, simply to maintain her balance.

'Mark, I...I want to go home,' she heard herself croak, 'back to London.'

'That's out of the question,' he said, his attention clearly on the printer he was now peering at with a frown. 'How much longer is this thing going to go on spewing out paper?'

'Until it's finished!' she shrieked, snapping completely. 'Mark, I want to go *home*!'

'And I've told you—it's out of the question,' he responded, his eyes steely as he returned his attention to her. 'Tell me, Lucy, is there some sort of time-scale involved in whatever it is you've been hatching out in that scheming little mind of yours?'

'Time-scale?' she echoed dazedly.

'You heard,' he rasped. 'Why the sudden rush to get back to London?'

She looked at him in disbelieving horror. 'You're determined to believe that I'm plotting against you in some way, aren't you? I . . . I just don't understand you.'

'You certainly don't if you think you'll succeed in settling your imagined juvenile scores with me by leaping into my arms and then out for whatever devious purpose you have in mind,' he snarled.

'Just listen to yourself, for heaven's sake!' she choked, devastated. 'You sound paranoid! I happen to have grown up—you obviously haven't!'

'So why did you fall into my arms with such remarkable ease?'

'I could ask you the same question!'

'You could—but it's no answer!'

'For heaven's sake, Mark, I . . . I gave in to a strong physical attraction—one that I'm sure shocked you as much as it did me,' she stammered hoarsely. 'And it's something I regret every bit as much as you do.'

'But it's still there, isn't it, Lucy?' he demanded, 'that strong physical attraction.'

She felt drained and mentally battered, but there was defiance in her eyes as they rose to his.

'Lucy,' he warned softly, 'I'll only feel obliged to prove just how alive it still is if you're foolish enough to try denying it.'

'All right—I shan't deny it,' she muttered defeatedly.

'So... why do you want to leave?'

'Because I'm not happy,' she replied with the candour of total defeat.

'Perhaps I should try to remedy that,' he stated quietly.

'It wouldn't help,' she said, a sudden tightness constricting her breathing.

'But at least let me try,' he said, his tone curiously expressionless. 'Why don't you go and change? We'll find somewhere relaxed and friendly to eat.'

Her eyes widened a fraction: it was almost as though he was admitting that his previous choice of eating places had been the opposite.

'Don't you worry about the printer,' he continued, 'I'll see to it.'

The trouble with being so helplessly in love as she was, Lucy told herself as she changed, was that any crumb of warmth, however suspect, had a dangerous effect. He had switched from snarling venom to quiet consideration in a matter of seconds—and all to make her happy, she pointed out grimly to herself... and she was supposed to swallow that without question! But one thing she hadn't forgotten was his cynical tirade against love during the journey down, when he had equated the power of making either heaven or hell of another's life with that of love... And now, having made her life such hell, he was toying with turning it into heaven—but why?

There was a bitter smile hovering on her lips as she went to join him. There was a terrible irony in the fact that his cynical decision to make her 'happy' could never work by dint of that very cynicism, and that her continuing misery would actually prove a source of comfort to her in that it would certainly allay any suspicions he might or might not have about her loving him.

They ate in a sprawling barn of a place which they happened on by chance. Its atmosphere more than matched that of the first place she remembered so fondly, especially when they became drawn into the exuberant celebrations of the tail-end of a wedding party.

Lucy knew that happiness was glowing in her face when she was dragged into the ring of cheering, clapping women encircling the group of men initiating a laughing Mark into the intricacies of a traditional dance; and knew, too, that it remained there as time and again the two of them were coaxed into active participation in the raucous celebrations.

It was one thing for the infectious happiness of a crowd of merrymakers to rub off on her, but quite another to feel that same happiness bubbling on within her long after she and Mark had parted company with them—and it was a realisation that disturbed her profoundly.

'Are you sure you're not cold?' Mark asked, the second time he had expressed concern for her welfare since they had left the restaurant and, at his suggestion, taken a walk along the darkened, windswept front to clear their heads.

Lucy shook her head. 'It's bliss breathing fresh air after the smell of those firecrackers—I nearly leapt out of my skin when they started letting them off.'

'It's quite some form of celebration,' he laughed. 'I doubt if my hearing will ever recover.'

Listening to the lazy lap of the waves against the rocks as they strolled on, Lucy felt a prickly unease begin to erode her glow of happiness. When he was relaxed and as companionable as this it was all too easy to love him, she warned herself in desperation, and far too easy to forget what she could never afford to forget.

'It was good to see you looking so happy,' he stated quietly.

Though there was no discernible barb in his words, she felt driven to disrupt this too dangerous harmony between them.

'Other people's happiness can be infectious,' she retorted stiffly.

'Lucy, I'm not deluding myself I was in any way the cause of it,' he said. 'I just liked seeing you happy.'

She tensed, his words disturbing her far beyond any meaning she could read into them.

'If you're so fond of seeing me happy, I suggest you stop dragging me off to eat in those soulless places you usually choose—they're guaranteed to dampen anyone's sense of enjoyment.'

'Never again—I promise.'

His reply threw her completely and her mind was in complete turmoil as her steps quickened towards the car.

'Mark—what made you choose them in the first place?' she asked with strained reluctance, halting as they reached the car.

'Lucy, don't let's argue,' he pleaded, turning her towards him and cupping her face in his hands.

'I wasn't arguing,' she protested unsteadily, resolution deserting her as her eyes became ensnared in the teasing softness of his. 'I was merely... It's raining!'

'So it is,' he murmured, making no attempt to move. 'You know, there's something about Spanish rain—I think I could get to prefer it to sunshine.'

She wanted to beg him to stop.

'That's just as well—seeing that it's done little else but rain since we've been here,' were the words that eventually came from her, forced and unsteady as every pulse in her body raced distortedly.

'Lucy, before we let the rain wash our slate clean, just tell me one thing—was there really no other reason than your being unhappy that made you want to leave?'

It was after her automatic and vehement shake of her head that a *frisson* of fear spread through her at the thought of what she might be admitting.

'I'll destroy you if there was,' he told her, the glittering intensity of his eyes adding menace to the beguiling softness of his words. 'You know that, don't you, Lucy?'

'You're beginning to sound paranoid again,' she heard herself respond, words that should have censured sounding more like a declaration of love to her appalled ears.

Laughing, he swung her up in his arms and spun them around. 'It's time I got you home before the pair of us drown!'

Once in the car, he drew her head against his shoulder and started up the engine, his arm still around her.

'You know,' he chuckled, 'I've never gone in for automatic cars—right now I'm just beginning to see that they might have their advantages.'

'If you like, I'll change gear,' offered Lucy, a feeling of delirious intoxication filling her at the thought of her being the first person he had ever wanted to keep his arm around while driving.

'Oh, no,' he murmured. 'I want to get us home in one piece.' He tilted back her head and brushed his lips lightly over hers. 'And as quickly as I possibly can.'

By the time they reached their destination the electrifying tension between them was such that the intoxication of happiness she had tried to restrain spilled over as they wrestled their way through the house towards the bedroom, splashing out in the rash delight of laughter to the sounds of the outrageously explicit murmurings pouring from lips that explored ravenously against her whenever they touched.

It was her complete lack of any previous experience that had in a strange way protected her from what she discovered in his arms that night. Love having stripped all inhibition from her, her body had yielded unreservedly to his, abandoning itself in unquestioning ardour to the explosive delights unleashed in it by his.

But that night he introduced the new dimension of tenderness to the passionate intensity of their lovemaking—and that was her undoing. Before, overwhelmed by the physical perfection of their lovemaking, she had been lulled into deluding herself that this was enough. But it was that unexpected tenderness, so achingly close to the love she craved, that at first enchanted her and then gradually began tormenting her with consciousness of just how much she was being denied.

When at last he slept in her arms she gazed down at the chiselled perfection of his sleeping features and found herself rehearsing the words that would tell him of the truth she had already imparted to him in every way except words. And when those words were so fully rehearsed that the temptation to wake him and speak them became too unbearable, she gently eased him from her and walked to the window, welcoming the coolness of the glass against her cheek as she closed her eyes and her mind to all save the soft patter of the still-falling rain.

He came to her on soundless bare feet.

'Now that I've stayed, you're abandoning me,' he teased sleepily, his arms enfolding her from behind. 'Is this your way of telling me I've overstayed my welcome?' There was confident laughter in words as he rubbed his chin against the top of her head.

She didn't have to tell him he could never outstay his welcome with her, she accepted fatalistically, because he seemed already to know it.

'I wanted to see if there was a moon,' she lied, turning in his arms and placing her own around his neck.

'To wish on?' he asked huskily, his lips nuzzling against her cheek.

'I didn't know you could wish on the moon,' she whispered, her heart feeling as though it must break.

'Tonight you can wish on whatever you choose,' he promised hoarsely as his lips hotly claimed hers.

'Eat your toast,' Mark ordered, drifting through the bathroom and into his own room, reappearing seconds later struggling into a shirt. 'I'll have you know I spent gruelling hours slaving over making it.'

'Over making toast?' enquired Lucy, and with considerable difficulty, given that her heart and just about every other part of her had been turning riotous somersaults ever since the moment he had awakened her with a prolonged kiss and the announcement that he had brought her breakfast.

'Over making toast,' he confirmed with a growl, disappearing once again.

'The coffee's delicious,' she called after his departing figure.

'So, what's wrong with the toast?' he demanded, this time reappearing donning a pair of trousers.

'Nothing—there's just too much of it,' she replied, laughter in her voice. How could she possibly be expected to eat toast when she was feeling like this?

'My, but you can be an ungrateful brat at times,' he sighed piously, sitting down on the bed and proceeding to get into his socks.

'Mark, wouldn't it have been easier for you simply to get dressed all in one go in your own room?'

'Yes.'

She leaned back against the pillows, love and a strange contentment suffusing her as she sipped her coffee and waited for him to continue.

His eyes rose from his task, locking with hers.

'Perhaps my being so companionable and getting dressed in here wasn't such a good idea after all.' His words were teasing, but neither his tone nor his eyes were in the least.

'Do you really have to go?' pleaded Lucy, her arms automatically reaching out to him.

He moved towards her, then caught her fiercely in his arms.

'There are too many people involved for me to cancel,' he whispered huskily.

'I know—it was stupid of me to ask,' she choked, burying her face against the familiar, scented warmth of him.

He was shaking his head as he reluctantly drew her from him.

'No...it wasn't in the least stupid. Lucy, I...' He broke off, rising to his feet. 'We simply haven't time to talk right now,' he muttered, his tone oddly strained. 'I'm not likely to be back until late this evening—but after today all we'll have are a few loose ends to tie up while we wait for the verdict...and plenty of time for ourselves.' He began walking towards the door. 'You won't forget that the bank's sending around a car for you at eleven?'

'I shan't forget,' she replied, trying hard not to be hurt by his sudden restraint.

'It's best if we get all the relevant taxes on the property up to date before these plans go through... Just sign whatever cheques the bank manager asks you to—the lawyer will have provided him with the figures. And don't forget to take your passport along with you—in case they require it for identification purposes.'

'Don't worry—I'll take my passport and I'll try not to make a hash of signing a few cheques, I promise.'

'I didn't mean to nag,' he apologised sheepishly.

'I didn't mean to imply you were,' she murmured, his words acting as a miraculous balm on her fluctuating confidence. 'I just don't want you to have anything on your mind at this meeting... Good luck with the plans.'

'Thanks,' he murmured, opening the door. 'And if you're wondering why I'm not kissing you goodbye,' he added with a rueful chuckle, 'it's because I don't trust either of us.'

For a long while after the door had closed behind him, Lucy remained sitting up in bed, hugging her knees and gazing into space while her mind took off on a journey of the wildest speculation. But was the idea of his loving her any crazier than that of their becoming lovers would have seemed only weeks ago?

She closed her eyes, suddenly fearful of the hopes and dreams coursing through her unfettered. Last night she had wished on the moon, she reminded herself wryly, and now she was entertaining lunatic thoughts!

But as she showered and dressed she found her mood swinging so wildly between hope and despair that for her sanity's sake she was forced to gather up all those dreams and fears and relegate them to the recesses of her mind. Grasping desperately at anything that would keep her occupied, she tidied the office, arranging and rearranging items already immaculately in place and then indulging in several minutes of welcome preoccupation when she thought she had misplaced her passport. She found it in the handbag she hadn't used since the journey down and in doing so was provided with further welcome distraction by coming across the bundle of letters erroneously delivered to her neighbour's postbox. She pulled a small face as she sifted through them and decided they wouldn't distract her very long. Apart from a birthday card from an old schoolfriend, the rest looked uninterestingly like circulars—all but two were.

Her body tensing in horror, she broke off from reading the first to tear open the second. Both letters were from the Inland Revenue; the first, dated almost three months earlier than the second, was an official demand for immediate payment of tax due on her earnings from her writing. The letter went on to inform her that she had incurred penalties for having failed to submit a declaration of her additional earnings in the relevant tax year.

It was the second letter that panicked her completely. The penalties had been increased even further and she was required to attend a meeting to discuss immediate payment. The letter went on to point out the range of measures open to the Inspector of Taxes to obtain the amount due, any or all of which would be considered should she fail to attend the meeting at the date and time specified. That date, she realised with mounting horror, was the following day—at three o'clock in the afternoon.

CHAPTER TEN

'So—HOW did Mark react when you told him?' After posing the question, Sarah Mitson leaned back in the chair in Lucy's living-room and closed her eyes as though in prayer.

'Sarah, how could I tell him? He took me there to keep me out of harm's way while his father was convalescing,' muttered Lucy wearily. 'The instant I opened those wretched letters I could see the headlines flashing before my eyes—"Sick Tycoon's Stepdaughter on Tax Fraud Charges" being one of the milder ones.'

Sarah maintained that almost prayerful silence.

'If they'd put a distraint, or whatever it's called, on my earnings, James *could* have got to learn of it,' continued Lucy, her defensive words sounding suspect even to her own accommodating ears.

'So—you didn't tell Mark,' stated Sarah quietly.

'He was at an important meeting all day and if I'd waited for him to return I might not have been able to get a plane back in time.' She glared across at Sarah, feeling betrayed by her friend's almost hostile attitude. 'OK, I admit it,' she exploded bitterly, 'I chickened out of facing him and ran!'

'You haven't told me how you got on with the tax people,' coaxed Sarah, changing the subject with painstaking tact.

Lucy gave a half-hearted shrug. 'Mrs Dixon kindly rang them and explained about my post going astray,' she muttered. 'They've waived the penalties and given me time to pay.'

'Well, at least that's something,' sighed Sarah, not sounding entirely convinced. She hesitated before continuing. 'What about work—will you be coming in tomorrow?'

'If you mean will I be coming in to clear my desk before Mark gets back—the answer is yes,' replied Lucy with a grim smile.

'Lucy, you can't simply go on letting him believe you're some sort of congenital idiot,' groaned Sarah. 'Half, if not most, of your problems stem from the fact that you've always been too proud to explain yourself to him, yet his having the opinion he does of you can hardly do much for your pride anyway.'

'Let's face it, Sarah, I knew I'd have to pay tax on the money I earned from my writing. It was my own stupid fault that I didn't get it sorted out ages ago.' She hesitated, sighing before continuing. 'One thing you forgot to ask me was where I got the money for the fare.'

'Take it as asked now,' said Sarah, her tone decidedly apprehensive.

'I spun the Spanish bank manager a yarn about needing to fly back here on urgent business for Mark. He kindly made all the arrangements and got me to Alicante airport.'

'And the money?'

'I signed a company cheque.

'You forged Mark's signature?' shrieked Sarah.

'Sarah, even I wouldn't try that with a bank manager peering over my shoulder,' pointed out Lucy wryly. 'Mark had already made me a signatory.'

'I suppose it's the same difference, though,' groaned Sarah. 'Would that be classed as embezzlement?'

'My, but you're a comfort to have around,' giggled Lucy, then promptly burst into tears. 'Sarah, what am I going to do?' she pleaded raggedly.

'Mark would never take action over your signing that cheque,' protested Sarah.

'That's not what I meant. I ... oh, what's the use?'

'Lucy, whatever happened between the two of you in Spain is your own business,' said Sarah quietly. 'But something tells me it's about time you faced up to Mark and told him the truth. And I don't just mean about the tax fiasco—I mean all of it, going back to the year dot if necessary. You owe it to your pride simply to let him know how wrong he was about you.'

'He'd shout me down before I got a couple of words out,' muttered Lucy, while the remnants of her pride clamoured for her to agree.

'So you shout even louder—you've nothing to lose,' urged Sarah. 'And while we're facing facts, are you absolutely sure about chucking in the job?'

'Sarah, you know how I feel about working for Waterford's,' protested Lucy.

'Yes, I do. But if your suspicions are right, Mark will sabotage your attempts to find work anywhere else.'

'Not this time, he won't,' said Lucy, a bitter, aching sense of loss threatening to smother her. 'I think you'll find he can't get rid of me quick enough.'

'If that's the case—you'll stay,' announced Sarah firmly. 'And there's no need to look at me as though I've flipped,' she added gently. 'You'll need the sort of salary you're getting to pay off your tax debts and keep you going until you're secure enough in your writing to be able to walk out and not be dependent on Mark not giving you a lousy reference.'

There was silence between them for several seconds.

'Sarah, you're right on just about every score,' sighed Lucy eventually. 'But it's one thing being perfectly aware of what I should do and another entirely finding what it takes to do it.'

'You've got what it takes,' declared Sarah. 'And by the time Mark returns, we'll make sure you don't have a single doubt left that you have.'

By the time Lucy reached the office the following morning, there wasn't a single coherent thought in her head, on top of which she was feeling crushed and devastated.

Of course Sarah had been right—but did it really matter? She stood in the middle of the room, her gaze fixed almost hypnotically on the door of Mark's office, as she asked herself if anything would ever really matter again. While part of her willed the door to fly open and for him to be standing there, another part became almost detachedly preoccupied with finding a word that would exactly describe her present state of mind . . . the state of mind she had been in since leaving the villa.

Though she tried to shy away from it, she found herself remembering the agony of loss she had felt when her father had died. Frightened and half ashamed at such thoughts, she began remonstrating angrily with herself. Mark had never been hers to lose, she reminded herself bitterly. The fact that she loved him was irrelevant because to him it had been no more than a temporary sharing of passion, doubtless no different from that he had shared with countless others. But even knowing that didn't alter the fact that, since her leaving the villa, there hadn't been a moment during which she hadn't ached, both physically and mentally, with an unbearable sense of loss.

Her eyes still trained on the door, her mind began conjuring up a picture of him opening it and standing before her.

'You're wrong, Sarah,' she protested in vehement desperation. 'I'll never find what it takes to...' Her words choked to a stricken halt as the door opened and he was standing there.

In her mind's picture he had been dressed in jeans and a sweater and there had been tenderness in his smile. In reality he was dark-suited, and there was no trace of any sort of smile on the drawn grimness of his features.

'Who were you talking to?' he demanded, frowning as he glanced around the room behind her.

Had her legs not turned to immovable lead, Lucy would have turned and fled.

'Mark, I...what...where's your car?' she floundered, and saw that the words she had finally produced appeared to have startled him almost as much as they had her.

'My car?' he echoed, momentarily thrown. 'I suppose it's at Alicante airport where I left it—why?'

Why? The question reverberated in her mind as the rest of her turned to lead. Just as everything seemed about to seize up on her completely, she heard Sarah's frantic exhortations ringing in her head.

'Mark, I can explain,' she blurted out. 'I want to tell you everything!'

'Don't!' he cut in sharply. 'I don't want any explanations. I——'

'You're going to hear them anyway,' she cried—if she didn't do it here and now, she never would! 'For a start, I didn't set fire to the school!' She shook her head frustratedly, then quickly corrected herself. 'Well, I did, actually—but it was an accident. I dropped a candle and——'

'Lucy——'

'And I didn't deliberately wreck your car, either,' she ploughed on as though driven. 'I thought that Perry— your neighbour's dog—had been run over. I'd no idea he had fits and when I...' He moved, interrupting the manic flow of her words by folding his arms and leaning his tall body against the door-frame and regarding her with a look of wary detachment.

'Lucy, give me some credit,' he drawled. 'Irritatingly unforthcoming you may have been as a child, but I never once regarded you as an arsonist or a car wrecker—despite your apparent determination that I should.'

'But you treated me as though you did,' she protested faintly as she found herself having to fight off a desperate need to race to him and fling herself in his arms.

'As I said, you seemed determined I should think the worst of you—I simply obliged,' he replied. 'But don't think I'm going to oblige now by letting you distract me by all this harping on about the past.'

'I'm not trying to distract you,' she protested weakly. 'Mark . . . I'm simply trying to explain.'

'OK—explain.'

'I didn't tell you about my writing——'

'Oh, for God's sake, I've had enough of this!' he exploded, straightening and dragging his fingers impatiently through his hair. 'Lucy, when I came haring back here after you, I promised myself that there would be no more of these ritual rehashings of the past—not even the immediate past!'

His words hit her like a physical blow. Already she had been relegated to his past—albeit his immediate past.

'But you make it damned near impossible! I was prepared to put aside the fact that I had asked you on numerous occasions to tell me the truth, and even that you cited unhappiness as your only reason for wanting to leave——'

'It *was* my only reason!' she exclaimed indignantly. 'Well . . . it was at the time.'

'I take it I'm now supposed to ask you what it changed to,' he stated frigidly. 'OK, Lucy—why did you take off like a thief in the night?'

'Because I had an appointment with my local tax office at three o'clock yesterday afternoon,' she chanted woodenly, her head reeling. 'And if I didn't turn up——'

'Forget I asked! I don't want to hear another word of this!' he bellowed, stepping back into his office and slamming the door shut behind him.

She could have rehearsed it for a month and it never would have come out right, she thought distractedly. It was the sudden sting of tears on her cheeks that switched her feelings to a churning mixture of rage and hopelessness. Nobody was ever going to have the power to reduce her to this again, she vowed, scrubbing furiously at her cheeks. And though she would have given her right arm for it to be otherwise, Sarah was right—he would have to be blind not to realise she was in love with him. Yet, even knowing that, he still hadn't been prepared to let her redeem what scrap of her pride she could by hearing her out! Well, he was going to hear her out, even if she had to bludgeon him over the head to keep him still enough to do so!

Her face grim with resolution, she marched to the door of his office and flung it open, jarring her arm with the force she then used to hurl it shut behind her.

'This shouldn't take long, but I don't really care if it takes all day... Mark?'

Where the hell was he?

'Yes?'

She spun round to where his voice had come from, desperately trying to maintain the momentum of her anger as she felt it weaken at the sight of him stretched out on the black leather sofa in a far corner of the room.

'For once in my life I'm going to have my say,' she announced, paradoxically almost managing to hate him for the rage of love aroused in her at the sight of the weariness now so starkly visible on his features as she strode determinedly to the sofa.

'If you say so,' he muttered, not even bothering to look in her direction.

'I do say so. But it's been so long since I've had a chance to have my say that I've probably forgotten how!'

'I'm sure it will come back to you,' he murmured with biting sarcasm. 'But why not save yourself all that effort by simply not bothering?' He sat up, still not even glancing in her direction. 'I suppose the most comforting thing about you, Lucy, is that, given enough rope, you inevitably oblige by hanging yourself.'

'Mark, I'm not interested in your sneering comments,' she stated tonelessly, struggling to blank her mind of all save the task before her. 'I've come to say something and I intend saying it.'

'So you keep telling me,' he sighed. 'But it's no more than yet another variation on the same old theme.' He gave a bitter laugh. 'To think I'd actually begun believing you were what you kept claiming to be—a rational adult! How wrong could I be? Scrape at your surface, Lucy, and what do we find? A selfish, confused fifteen-year-old. Such self-centred angst in a fifteen-year-old is irritating, but fairly predictable...in a twenty-three-year-old it's downright dangerous.'

'Dangerous?' she croaked, stunned. 'Mark, how could I ever be a danger to you?'

'How indeed?' he murmured wryly, his eyes briefly meeting hers. 'Though I was thinking more in terms of your being a danger to yourself.'

'If I really were the way you see me, I'd have to agree,' she said quietly, the need to put her case to him with dignity suddenly of paramount importance to her. 'In fact, I'd say I was unbalanced.'

He glanced up at her again, his look slightly startled.

'Yet how do I convince you that I'm neither dangerous nor unbalanced when, in trying to do so, I immediately condemn myself by referring to the past?'

'Lucy, I doubt whether I'm going to have either the physical or mental stamina required for this,' he sighed, dragging his hands wearily down his face, 'but I suppose I have no choice but to give it a try. I suggest you sit down and get on with it.'

Lucy began glancing nervously around her, looking for a chair small enough for her to drag over.

'Damn it, Lucy, this thing was designed to take four,' he snapped, pointedly moving himself further towards one corner of the sofa.

Lucy seated herself at the opposite end, trying to look composed as her mind unkindly began dwelling on times when she had lain locked in his arms.

'Right—now that we're both sitting in a semblance of comfort,' he drawled, 'perhaps you'd care to get on with it.'

She got started only with considerable difficulty, having to contend with both her mind and her tongue seizing up with apprehension. But as her words grew less faltering, so her mind began applying itself with meticulous thoroughness to its task. Never once allowing herself to forget that this was her final chance to clear the misunderstandings of the past, she candidly and objectively covered any detail she felt might be relevant, steeling herself not to be distracted by his frequent gestures of ill-concealed impatience.

'Lucy, I can't blame you for reacting as you did at the time and letting me think the worst,' he said at one point. 'I realise the blame is mine for——'

'I'm not asking you to blame yourself,' she protested frustratedly. 'That's not why I'm telling you all this—can't you understand?'

'Can't *you* understand that I simply don't attach the same importance to it that you obviously do?' he muttered. 'It's all dead and buried in the past, for heaven's sake!'

'But it isn't!' she cried, her resolve threatening to desert her as she began to believe she was simply wasting her breath—perhaps their personalities were just too different for him ever to be able to understand what she was getting at. 'Mark, can't you see that it's what colours your entire attitude to me?' she pleaded. 'If you hadn't such a negative opinion of me, would you really have felt obliged to keep such close tabs on me while your father was recuperating?'

He shrugged. 'I really don't see what any of this has to do with your upping and leaving Spain as you did.'

Desperate to mask her hurt at his deliberate avoidance of answering her question, she continued, telling him about her writing and the misdirected letters from the Inland Revenue; but her heart was no longer in her task.

'The letters had completely slipped my mind,' she related tonelessly. 'I only came across them when I was looking for my passport to take to the bank.'

'The morning of the day you left,' he stated, no hint of any question·in his grimly uttered statement. 'I suppose that was as good an excuse as any for taking off.'

'Excuse?' she croaked, stunned by the harshness of his tone. 'Mark, I panicked. I know it sounds ridiculous now, but I got it into my head that if I didn't keep that appointment your father would somehow get to hear about it.'

'The chances that he would have are so remote as to be almost non-existent,' pointed out Mark frigidly. 'But even if he had, can you honestly envisage his having a relapse over your owing a bit of back tax?'

'I told you I panicked,' she rounded on him in desperation. 'That's the effect you have on me! That's why...oh, why am I even bothering with this?'

'I've no idea,' he exploded, rising to his feet and glowering down at her. 'I told you I wasn't looking for explanations, but you wouldn't listen. No—you had to have your say!' He rammed one hand in his pocket and dragged the other distractedly through his hair. 'You keep on about the effect I have on you, but you're not so bad at screwing things up yourself! Not that I'm complaining, mind you,' he raged. 'In fact, I should be down on my knees thanking you!'

'So—if it wasn't to wring an explanation out of me,' exploded Lucy, leaping to her feet, 'what did bring you back here?'

'That's the question you should have asked me at the start,' he snarled.

'I don't know why I bothered asking it at any point— not when the answer's so blindingly obvious,' she choked out, stumbling past him in her race to get to the door before she went completely to pieces.

'Perhaps you'd care to enlighten me as to that blindingly obvious answer,' he rasped, catching her by the arm and halting her flight.

'I suppose it must have been a little difficult for you deciding exactly which way I'd wreak my revenge on you!

Had you visions of me setting fire to one of the Waterford's buildings as you dashed back? Or perhaps it was of me seeking out another crook with whom to hit the headlines? You didn't honestly expect me to swallow that rubbish about never believing I did any of those things deliberately, did you?'

It was the appalling realisation that any moment now she would be incapable of controlling either her words or her actions that gave her the strength to tear free and race to the door.

'Just where the hell do you think you're going?' he snarled, catching up with her.

'I...I have to let the switchboard know we're back,' she gabbled, terrified by the process of complete disintegration she sensed had begun in her.

'Don't bother,' he snapped. 'We're returning to Spain on the first available flight.'

'No,' she choked weakly, wrenching open the door.

'You seem to forget—I have business to complete.'

'Mark, why are you doing this to me?' she whispered, her head dropping defeatedly.

'Doing what to you, Lucy?' he demanded harshly. 'We've both achieved what we set out to do here—you to sort out your taxes and me to stop you committing arson, or whatever—so now it's back to business.'

'You still don't believe me,' she protested, stunned bewilderment in her eyes as they rose to his.

'Why should my believing you be so important to you?' he demanded, his eyes holding hers in blatant challenge.

'You already know why,' she replied without flinching, her pride putting up a last-ditch stand as though sensing its imminent destruction.

'Do I, Lucy?' he asked with steely softness. 'Perhaps I need to be told—not about how I confused you and tied you up in knots years ago, but what you actually feel towards me here and now.'

There were all sorts of thoughts chasing through Lucy's mind as she gazed up into the implacable harshness of his face, but the overriding feeling within her was one almost of relief. It was the utter callousness with which he was prepared to strip her of her last shreds of pride that would paradoxically ensure she retained it.

'You need to be told, Mark? Then you shall be told,' she stated witheringly. 'I love you. It doesn't say much for me that I love a man sadistic enough to demand that I say in words what he already hasn't a single doubt about... What sort of pervert are you, that you would want to humiliate me like this?'

'The sort of pervert who's realised that our past relationship, for differing reasons, looms like a mountain between us!' he raged, the weight of her body slamming shut the door as he lunged at her and grasped her by the shoulders. 'The pervert who was prepared to admit that I could be more honest with you than you were with me—but you wouldn't listen.'

Panicked by the rage surging in him, Lucy began kicking out at his legs in an effort to free herself, a move he countered simply by leaning even more of his weight on her and almost knocking the breath from her.

'How do you think I felt when you suddenly upped and left like that?' he roared.

'You weren't interested in hearing why,' protested Lucy, choking not only from his weight but from the unbearable longings his suffocating nearness aroused in her.

'No—because I knew that we'd end up yelling at one another, neither of us asking the right questions or even giving honest answers to the wrong ones.'

'Who's to say what the right ones are?' she choked.

'I asked you the right one not so long ago and you called me a sadistic pervert for my pains,' he sighed. 'I'm sure you haven't forgotten that first place we stopped at in Spain and how much you enjoyed the atmosphere there.'

Completely thrown by this change in his mood and those baffling words, Lucy tried to pull back from him simply to be able to glimpse the expression on his face, but he blocked her attempt.

'Yet when I deliberately kept you away from such places, you didn't even query it at the time.'

'What would you have answered if I had?' she asked, her lungs gulping at air as he eased the force of his weight from her to gaze down at her.

'I hope I would have been honest enough to admit that seeing your happiness frightened me.'

'Why should it frighten you?' she whispered hoarsely.

'Lucy, we always talk as though you were a small child when our paths first crossed,' he sighed, 'but you weren't; you were a beautiful young creature hovering on the threshold of womanhood.'

'You haven't answered my question,' she croaked, the effect of his words almost suffocating.

'No—but it's a beginning,' he muttered, taking her by the hand and leading her back to the sofa. He pulled her down beside him, immediately releasing her hand. 'I was the first man you ever looked at with the eyes of a woman,' he stated flatly.

And the only one, she admitted silently to herself as she tried to steel herself for what might come.

'Unfortunately it was with those same eyes that you always looked at me, no matter how much I refused to accept that fact or you tried to disguise it.'

'Why are you saying all this now?' she asked, fear prickling on her skin and chilling her voice.

'For the same reason that you felt somehow compelled to tell me the truth about yourself then,' he replied, 'except that you weren't prepared to tell me the whole truth.'

'But you are,' she stated hollowly.

'As much of it as I've been able to admit to myself,' he replied, then added even more confusingly, 'for a while, when you were about seventeen, we got on relatively well.'

'Yes, when your father and my mother lived in London for a few months,' she muttered, her tension betrayed in her tone as she added bitterly, 'but things reverted to their usual unpleasantness once they'd gone.'

'Their presence had nothing to do with it,' he said. 'It's just that it was around then that I began to suspect that you might have something to do with my apparent inability to fall in love.'

He gave soft chuckle of genuine amusement at her look of wide-eyed bemusement.

'Don't misunderstand me, I wouldn't have lost any sleep over the thought of never falling in love—it was the vague idea that you were somehow linked up with it that I didn't relish.'

'There was nothing vague about your behaviour towards me,' Lucy reminded him with ill-disguised bitterness.

'No—and you weren't very good at masking your hurt,' he muttered. 'In fact, you never really did learn to hide your feelings from me... not that it consciously bothered me then. But we both know it was only when I returned this time that everything about you started to bother me so badly.'

Of course she knew it, and had spotted it instantly, she thought in hurt and bitterly confused silence.

'Would it surprise you to hear that when you told me that pack of lies about George I was almost over the moon?'

'No—I'm sure it must have been quite a relief to think yourself finally rid of me,' she retorted coldly, yet again astounded by his callousness.

'Oh, no—I had the problem of being almost eaten up with jealousy until I managed to convince myself I wouldn't have too much difficulty winning you back from him.'

'Mark, what on earth are you talking about?' she demanded, in her perplexity recoiling just that little bit further from him on the sofa.

'I'm talking about my side of our problematical relationship,' he retorted with a shrug. 'I'm talking about seeing you struggle into womanhood with eyes only for me; about refusing to admit to myself that I wanted to shove you out into the world so that you could grow up and learn that puppy love is a stage you go through and then leave behind and which has nothing to do with adult love!'

'You think that what I feel for you is nothing more than puppy love?' she exclaimed in stunned disbelief.

'Lucy, as far as I can see you've never looked past me. You've had no experience with other men.'

'What was I supposed to do, alley-cat around the place for a few years so that my lack of experience wouldn't make you feel uncomfortable?'

'Lucy, I——'

'I *have* been out in the world! I *have* been involved with other men, but there was no way I could have loved any of them! And if you're saying I should have leapt into bed with a few of them, just to——'

'Lucy, stop this!' he yelled, hauling her across his lap and into his arms. 'Why didn't you let me do things my way? Why did you have to throw me by asking me about my bloody car instead of me? Why did you insist on talking round in circles instead of letting me do what I'd come here to do?'

'What exactly was it you came here to do?' she asked in a small, tentative voice, while she tried to ignore the sudden frenzied pounding of her heart.

'To take you in my arms and tell you I love you,' he groaned exasperatedly, as though she should already have known the answer. 'Though I'm afraid I didn't get around to thinking about what I was going to say after that.'

'Well, I suggest you get on with it,' she said in a peculiarly choked voice.

'What do you think I've been trying to do?' he protested. 'All that comes out is gibberish, thanks to the years of practice I've put in not even admitting to myself that one of these days I would lose my heart to you.'

'It wasn't the gibberish I was suggesting you got on with,' she chided, her lips giving in to the temptation to do a little exploring around the vicinity of his jawline. 'It was the putting-your-arms-around-me-and-telling-me-you-love-me bit that I had in mind.'

'Oh, that bit,' he murmured, then chuckled softly. 'But I've already got my arms around you.'

'Mark!'

'I love you,' he whispered, no trace of laughter in his voice. 'Lucy, I lied to us both when I said I was taking you to Spain to keep an eye on you. By kidding myself that all you had was an adolescent crush on me, I could avoid examining my feelings for you. Your happiness frightened me in that it was almost childlike in its intensity... hell, I'm back to spouting gibberish again,' he groaned, burying his face against hers.

'It doesn't matter when I first started loving you,' she whispered pleadingly. 'It's a woman who loves you now—not an adolescent butterfly flitting from one experience to the next.'

'In my heart of hearts I knew that,' he muttered, 'but it was only once you left me that I had no option but to stop deluding myself and face the fact that I want you beside me always.'

'You're making me cry,' she protested, clinging to him in a confusion of happiness almost too much for her to bear.

'I'll make you cry bucketfuls if you start telling me you're not ready for marriage,' he growled contentedly.

'It was only George I said that about,' she hiccuped in protest.

'Are you certain that swine really doesn't exist?' he chuckled.

'You're the only man who's ever existed for me,' she vowed passionately.

'So—you'll marry me?'

Unable to speak, she nodded vigorously, burrowing her face against the vibrant warmth of his neck. 'I'm the happiest person in the world,' she wailed. 'I can't believe this is happening to me.'

'I love you, my darling Lucy,' he whispered, rocking her tenderly in his arms and chuckling softly to himself. 'But do you think you could manage to tone down this happiness of yours long enough for us to get to the airport and on to a plane?'

'Are we really going back to Spain today?' she croaked, stirring in his arms.

He nodded.

'I'm so glad. I know you have business there,' she added hastily.

'Very important business,' he murmured huskily. 'The business of going back to finish off what we began so shakily but which we'll continue with absolute confidence for the rest of our lives—the joyful business of discovering all those things we were so busy hiding from one another. I want to hold you in my arms and hear the rain beating against the windows as we catch up on all the words of love we once held back. I want to read the stories you've written and so wickedly kept secret from me.'

'I'll dedicate all the rest to you,' she promised, her eyes brimming over with love as she reached up to stroke his cheek.

'Wouldn't it be more appropriate to dedicate children's books to children?' he enquired, his eyes caressing hers.

'Perhaps that's one of the questions we'll be discussing in Spain,' she murmured tremulously, happiness almost stifling her.

'Lucy, have you any idea how much I love you?' he whispered hoarsely.

She was still trying to come to terms with the devastating effects of those and all his other words when he suddenly rose, tipping her off his lap and bringing a squeak of indignation from her.

'Sorry,' he murmured, grinning down at her as he helped her to her feet, 'but I think it's about time we said our goodbyes here and got ourselves back to our own private paradise where we'll have all the time in the world to ourselves.' He drew her against him, his lips teasing softly against hers. 'The day before yesterday I couldn't risk kissing you goodbye because I knew I'd never want to leave your arms... Tomorrow morning we'll be in one another's arms, just as we shall be for all the tomorrows to come.'

There were no words she could find to match the beauty of his at that moment, but as he took her by the hand and led her towards their future she knew she had all their tomorrows in which to discover them.

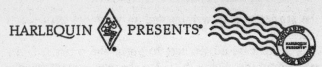

HARLEQUIN ◆ PRESENTS®

Harlequin Presents hopes you have enjoyed your year in Europe. If you missed any of the exciting countries on the tour, here is your opportunity to complete your collection:

Greece	#1619	*The Alpha Man* by Kay Thorpe	$2.99 ☐
Italy	#1628	*Mask of Deception* by Sara Wood	$2.99 ☐
Germany	#1636	*Designed To Annoy* by Elizabeth Oldfield	$2.99 ☐
Spain	#1644	*Dark Sunlight* by Patricia Wilson	$2.99 ☐
Belgium	#1650	*The Bruges Engagement* by Madeleine Ker	$2.99 ☐
Italy	#1660	*Roman Spring* by Sandra Marton	$2.99 U.S. ☐ $3.50 CAN.☐
England	#1668	*Yesterday's Affair* by Sally Wentworth	$2.99 U.S. ☐ $3.50 CAN.☐
Portugal	#1676	*Sudden Fire* by Elizabeth Oldfield	$2.99 U.S. ☐ $3.50 CAN.☐
Cyprus	#1684	*The Touch of Aphrodite* by Joanna Mansell	$2.99 U.S. ☐ $3.50 CAN.☐
Denmark	#1691	*Viking Magic* by Angela Wells	$2.99 U.S. ☐ $3.50 CAN.☐
Switzerland	#1700	*No Promise of Love* by Lilian Peake	$2.99 U.S. ☐ $3.50 CAN.☐
France	#1708	*Tower of Shadows* by Sara Craven	$2.99 U.S. ☐ $3.50 CAN.☐

HARLEQUIN PRESENTS
NOT THE SAME OLD STORY!

TOTAL AMOUNT	$
POSTAGE & HANDLING	$
($1.00 for one book, 50¢ for each additional)	
APPLICABLE TAXES*	$ _____
TOTAL PAYABLE	$ _____
(check or money order—please do not send cash)	

To order, complete this form and send it, along with a check or money order for the total above, payable to Harlequin Books, to: **In the U.S.:** 3010 Walden Avenue, P.O. Box 9047, Buffalo, NY 14269-9047; **In Canada:** P.O. Box 613, Fort Erie, Ontario, L2A 5X3.

Name: _____

Address: _____ City: _____

State/Prov.: _____ Zip/Postal Code: _____

*New York residents remit applicable sales taxes.
Canadian residents remit applicable GST and provincial taxes.

HPPFE-F

MILLION DOLLAR SWEEPSTAKES (III)

No purchase necessary. To enter, follow the directions published. Method of entry may vary. For eligibility, entries must be received no later than March 31, 1996. No liability is assumed for printing errors, lost, late or misdirected entries. Odds of winning are determined by the number of eligible entries distributed and received. Prizewinners will be determined no later than June 30, 1996.

Sweepstakes open to residents of the U.S. (except Puerto Rico), Canada, Europe and Taiwan who are 18 years of age or older. All applicable laws and regulations apply. Sweepstakes offer void wherever prohibited by law. Values of all prizes are in U.S. currency. This sweepstakes is presented by Torstar Corp., its subsidiaries and affiliates, in conjunction with book, merchandise and/or product offerings. For a copy of the Official Rules send a self-addressed, stamped envelope (WA residents need not affix return postage) to: MILLION DOLLAR SWEEPSTAKES (III) Rules, P.O. Box 4573, Blair, NE 68009, USA.

EXTRA BONUS PRIZE DRAWING

No purchase necessary. The Extra Bonus Prize will be awarded in a random drawing to be conducted no later than 5/30/96 from among all entries received. To qualify, entries must be received by 3/31/96 and comply with published directions. Drawing open to residents of the U.S. (except Puerto Rico), Canada, Europe and Taiwan who are 18 years of age or older. All applicable laws and regulations apply; offer void wherever prohibited by law. Odds of winning are dependent upon number of eligibile entries received. Prize is valued in U.S. currency. The offer is presented by Torstar Corp., its subsidiaries and affiliates in conjunction with book, merchandise and/or product offering. For a copy of the Official Rules governing this sweepstakes, send a self-addressed, stamped envelope (WA residents need not affix return postage) to: Extra Bonus Prize Drawing Rules, P.O. Box 4590, Blair, NE 68009, USA.

SWP-H1294

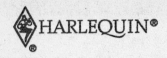 **HARLEQUIN®**

The proprietors of Weddings, Inc. hope you
have enjoyed visiting Eternity, Massachusetts.
And if you missed any of the exciting Weddings,
Inc. titles, here is your opportunity to complete
your collection:

Harlequin Superromance	#596	*Wedding Invitation* by Marisa Carroll	$3.50 U.S. ☐ $3.99 CAN. ☐	
Harlequin Romance	#3319	*Expectations* by Shannon Waverly	$2.99 U.S. ☐ $3.50 CAN. ☐	
Harlequin Temptation	#502	*Wedding Song* by Vicki Lewis Thompson	$2.99 U.S. ☐ $3.50 CAN. ☐	
Harlequin American Romance	#549	*The Wedding Gamble* by Muriel Jensen	$3.50 U.S. ☐ $3.99 CAN. ☐	
Harlequin Presents	#1692	*The Vengeful Groom* by Sara Wood	$2.99 U.S. ☐ $3.50 CAN. ☐	
Harlequin Intrigue	#298	*Edge of Eternity* by Jasmine Cresswell	$2.99 U.S. ☐ $3.50 CAN. ☐	
Harlequin Historical	#248	*Vows* by Margaret Moore	$3.99 U.S. ☐ $4.50 CAN. ☐	

HARLEQUIN BOOKS...
NOT THE SAME OLD STORY

TOTAL AMOUNT $
POSTAGE & HANDLING $
($1.00 for one book, 50¢ for each additional)
APPLICABLE TAXES* $ _____
TOTAL PAYABLE $ _____
(check or money order—please do not send cash)

To order, complete this form and send it, along with a check or money order for the
total above, payable to Harlequin Books, to: **In the U.S.:** 3010 Walden Avenue,
P.O. Box 9047, Buffalo, NY 14269-9047; **In Canada:** P.O. Box 613, Fort Erie, Ontario,
L2A 5X3.

Name: _____
Address: _____ City: _____
State/Prov.: _____ Zip/Postal Code: _____

*New York residents remit applicable sales taxes.
Canadian residents remit applicable GST and provincial taxes.

WED-F

This holiday, join four hunky heroes under
the mistletoe for

Christmas
Kisses

Cuddle under a fluffy quilt, with a cup of hot chocolate and these
romances sure to warm you up:

#561 HE'S A REBEL (also a Studs title)
Linda Randall Wisdom

#562 THE BABY AND THE BODYGUARD
Jule McBride

#563 THE GIFT-WRAPPED GROOM
M.J. Rodgers

#564 A TIMELESS CHRISTMAS
Pat Chandler

Celebrate the season with all four holiday books sealed with a
Christmas kiss—coming to you in December, only from
Harlequin American Romance!

CHRISTMAS STALKINGS

All wrapped up in spine-tingling packages, here are three books guaranteed to chill your spine...and warm your hearts this holiday season!

#302 THE KID WHO STOLE CHRISTMAS
Linda Stevens

#303 I'LL BE HOME FOR CHRISTMAS
Dawn Stewardson

#304 BEARING GIFTS
Aimée Thurlo

This December, fill your stockings with the "Christmas Stalkings"—for the best in romantic suspense. Only from